I0589076

Creative Texts Publishers products are available at special discounts for bulk purchase for sale promotions, premiums, fund-raising, and educational needs. For details, write Creative Texts Publishers, PO Box 50, Barto, PA 19504, or visit www.creativetexts.com

OZARK RETREAT
by Jerry D. Young
Published by Creative Texts Publishers
PO Box 50
Barto, PA 19504
www.creativetexts.com

The following is a work of fiction. Any resemblance to actual names, persons, businesses, and incidents is strictly coincidental. Locations are used only in the general sense and do not represent the real place in actuality.

ISBN: 978-0-692-50385-0

OZARK RETREAT

By
JERRY D. YOUNG

Copyright 2015
By JERRY D. YOUNG

Creative Texts Edition
Published by
CREATIVE TEXTS PUBLISHERS
BARTO, PA
www.creativetexts.com

OZARK RETREAT: PART ONE
PROLOGUE

Brady Collingsworth watched with interest as the two men approached the bank. They seemed to be more interested in what was behind them, than what was in front. Both wore camel trench coats and baseball caps. New York Yankees. Both had both their hands in their coat pockets. It just didn't seem that cool to Brady. Not cool enough to be dressed the way they were.

Picking up the microphone for the radio installed in the Suburban, Brady keyed it and said, "Barbara, get the police on the line and tell them there is some suspicious activity going on in front of Midland Bank."

"Sure thing, Boss. Don't do anything stupid," came the reply from the radio speaker.

"Stupid is relative," Brady said to no one as he exited the Suburban. He checked the street both ways and then sauntered across it, headed toward the bank entrance. He didn't go to the doors. Instead, he stopped at the edge of the rock façade of the building and squatted down. He took a small periscope from a pocket in the leather jacket he wore and took a long look around the corner of the entryway vestibule, through the glass doors, into the bank.

Sure enough, the two men were robbing the bank. One held a semi-auto pistol, and the other a short double barrel shotgun. Apparently the robbery was going okay. There had been no shots, and both men, while looking somewhat jittery, seemed calm enough.

Everyone he could see, except the perpetrators, was lying on the floor, arms outstretched. Brady stood, put his back against the wall of the building and waited. Hopefully the police would show up within a minute or two. Barbara could be pretty persuasive, when she set her mind to it.

But it was not to be. He heard the outer airlock door open. Spinning around, Brady stepped out, directly in front of the two men. A quick punch to the face of the man on Brady's left, and a kick to the side of the knee of the other one put both men down almost instantly.

Another moment and both were disarmed. Brady took the weapons and the trash bag of money and set them inside the airlock. Already people were approaching the doors from inside the bank.

Brady smiled and tipped his grey fedora to them. With that he turned around and left the vestibule. He immediately turned left and began to run. He saw a car pullout of a parking spot well down the block. He cut between two cars and ran into the street. The driver of the car slammed on the brakes and swerved to try to avoid Brady.

Spinning to one side, the car went slightly past him. The windows were all down in the car and Brady reached in, jabbing the driver in the throat with stiff fingers. The car was still rolling slowly as the man gasped for breath. The doors were unlocked and Brady opened it. Reaching across the driver's legs, Brady slammed the gearshift into park and the car came to an abrupt halt.

Keys in hand Brady backed out of the car and walked toward the police cruiser that had just pulled up. "Hi, Jonesy," Brady said as the officer rolled down his window. He handed Jonesy the keys he had pulled from the ignition of the robbers' getaway car.

"You might want some backup and an ambulance. There're three of them. Catch me down at the office in a little while and I'll give my statement. I have an appointment to keep."

Jonesy knew it wouldn't do any good to protest. He'd have to shoot Collingsworth to stop him, because he sure couldn't stop him physically. The man must have a dozen black belts in as many martial arts disciplines. He was the unarmed combat trainer for the city's small police force.

Jonesy was calling in for assistance as Brady walked back to his Suburban. People were standing in front of the bank, holding the robbers at the point of their own guns. When they saw him they started pointing and calling out to him.

Brady ignored the fuss and climbed into the Suburban. He pulled out of the parking space and drove away. He did have an appointment to get to. He didn't relish it. Twenty minutes later he was giving the bad news to Winchester Sanders, owner of Midland Bank, as well as two others in nearby cities.

"Yes, sir," Brady said, "They hit the bank just a little while ago. They didn't get away. Even if they don't squeal on your son, I have to give the police what I have. A crime has been committed and I have knowledge of it. I have to protect my license."

"I understand, Brady. I wasn't going to ask you to lie. I'm not sure I could have turned him in, but the fact that it is going to happen, I don't have a problem with. I'll cut you a check."

"Don't worry about it right now. We'll bill the bank in a few days. You need to concentrate on your son, and protecting your interests. When the news about your son's embezzlement and the attempted robbery to cover it up breaks, you could have trouble from the regulators and the patrons of the bank."

Winchester nodded. He stood up behind the desk and leaned forward to shake Brady's hand. "Thank you for keeping it quiet as long as you were able, and making it as easy as possible."

Brady was waiting for Detective Lieutenant Sandra Harrison when she arrived at his small office suite downtown. Barbara showed her right in. "Darn it, Brady! You have to quit leaving the scenes of crimes like that!"

"I told Jonesy I had an appointment to keep. Didn't he tell you?"

"Of course he told me. That doesn't make any difference. If it was anyone but me, they'd have you in the station, in a cell, along with the bank perps."

Brady leaned back in the leather upholstered chair and crossed his ankles on the corner of his desk. He tossed a file folder across the desk. Sandra caught it as it slid over the edge. "That's a copy of what I have. I wouldn't wait too long on Sonny. His father will most likely let him run, despite what he told me."

Sandra was reading the case file. "I've got to go," she said quickly and turned toward the door of the inner office. "You will come down to the station to make your statement. And that isn't a question."

Barbara stuck her head around the edge of the door after Sandra had left. "What's next, Boss?"

"What's pressing?"

"Harry is handling the small stuff. But the cult brain washing case has him spooked."

"Bring me the file."

CHAPTER ONE

Brady brought the Suburban to a halt by the fuel pumps of the Mini-Mart. It had been a long drive down to the Ozarks. He stretched before he began fueling the Suburban with gasoline. He looked around the area with interest. He switched the nozzle to the second tank the Suburban boasted and watched a tourist family take the place by storm. They all wore bright shirts, and khaki shorts. Sandals with socks. Camera straps were around every neck.

With a quick turn, he avoided one of the family from getting a shot of his face as they took pictures of him and the Suburban.

"Hey mister," said what looked to be a twelve year old boy came up to Brady. "Are you one of them survivalists we heard about down here?"

Brady smiled. "No, son, I'm not."

"Truck sure looks like it. But it isn't camouflaged so I guess it can't be. My daddy says they all drive big four wheel trucks and stuff and run around in camouflage shooting people they don't like with guns."

"I wouldn't know," Brady said. "I'm just a tourist like you."

"Don't look like a tourist, either," the youth said. But he turned around and ran over to his mother, who was holding out an ice cream bar for him.

Brady finished fueling. He'd paid with a credit card at the pump, but he went inside to take a look around after he'd cleaned the bugs off the windshield. Typical tourist area Mini-Mart. He got an Arizona bottled iced tea and went up to the counter to pay for the purchase. A pimply faced high school aged girl was behind the register.

"Hey, mister," she said as she took his money, "That's a nice truck. What lift do you have under it? My boyfriend has one with a twelve inch lift. It's cool."

"Two inches," Brady replied.

"That's not very much," she said. "You should lift it higher. Be a lot more cool."

"I'll keep it in mind. See you around." He picked up one of the free local maps.

Brady went back out to the Suburban and climbed in. He checked the itinerary Barbara had given him for the address of the hotel she had booked him. After unfolding the map, he found the address and headed for the hotel.

After settling in, and checking a few addresses and phone numbers in the telephone directory, Brady went scouting the town. Branson, Missouri, for a tourist town, he decided, wasn't too bad. Of course it was based on a down home, rural precept. They did it well, he thought.

He checked in to the Taney County Sheriff's office over in Forsyth after he checked into the hotel. He showed his detective's credentials and concealed carry permit. They weren't particularly happy with the idea, but didn't raise too many objections about him following up leads on his case. Brady did the same thing at the Branson City Police department. Again, he didn't get a hearty tourist's welcome, but the same offer of limited cooperation for cooperation on his part that the county had given him, and admonition to keep things legal.

Neither agency could provide him with any useable information on cults in the area. The only thing that came up was Survivalists. The boy at the Mini-Mart had mention survivalists. The hotel had a good internet connection. He used his computer with it to do some research on Survivalists. Brady found himself time and again leaving the specific search to go off on interesting tangents about the actual survival subjects.

After he logged off and had supper at one of the local restaurants, he decided to see a show. He was smiling when he returned to the hotel. Branson was a nice place to visit.

The following morning he went back to work. It involved casually probing questions of people that would be likely to have any contact with cults. Including Survivalists. They didn't seem to have any contact with the tourist part of Branson, except for the old time crafts presenters. It seemed a few survival minded people had asked those doing the demonstrations to give some private lessons. Many of the experts were happy to do so, for a fee.

Brady continued to ask questions, concentrating now on the locals. He just wasn't getting much information, and definitely not about cults, but the subject of Survivalists kept popping up.

Partly out of curiosity, partly from the growing belief that the cult his client had said his daughter had joined was a Survivalist Group, Brady began concentrating on that angle. He did two things, starting that second week of investigation. He booked a light charter aircraft at the Springfield-Branson Regional Airport for a flight over the area. He also contacted half a dozen real estate agencies in the area.

He took his digital mini-cam with him on the flight and recorded everything that looked like his recently developed ideas of a Survivalist compound. He included enough landmark shots to be able to pinpoint each one from the ground. It cost a bundle, but Brady felt it worth it. He had lots of possibilities to check out.

He told each of the real estate agents what he was looking for in the way of land acquisition. It was based on the same ideas he used for checking properties during the flight. One agent immediately asked if he was one of those 'Survivalists'.

"Why," Brady asked, "Does it make a difference?"

She shook her head. "No, not really, but it helps me define what to look for, for you. I sold one piece of property much like you say you want. When I asked them if they were, they denied it. My husband is a prepper and he was sure that's what the land was purchased for."

"The buyers put in a compound?" Brady asked.

"No, I haven't seen any development on the property at all. It's not too far from where I live. I could check with the owners and see if they are interested in selling."

"Let's leave that option open, but concentrate on properties already on, or coming onto the market."

Brady began checking the properties he'd seen from the air. He used the same spiel in each case. "Hi. I'm Brady. I'm thinking about buying a compound up here and wanted to meet my neighbors. Get some advice on wells and such. LaRhonda Richards put me onto the area." LaRhonda Richards was the woman he was trying to find.

Most of the places had locked gates or looked like they weren't currently inhabited. The ones with locked gates he knew he would just have to observe until he could catch someone arriving or leaving. He hoped he wouldn't have to do that. He could, but it was tiresome work.

The real estate agents began contacting him the third week he was in the area. A couple of them had access to some of the locked properties. They were up for sale. He kept looking. Brady was about to decide to start surveillance on the other locked down properties when he noticed the person he was talking to at one of the sites he'd found from the air reacted to his use of the name LaRhonda.

The fellow didn't say yea or nay about her, but Brady knew the signs. The man knew her. Brady actually got quite a bit of useful information about building in the area before he used LaRhonda's name. The man shut down then and made an excuse to go back inside the confines of the compound.

It was only a matter of time now that he had location pinpointed. He could concentrate on this compound. Brady didn't cancel the real estate agents' searches, but he wasn't quite sure why.

It wasn't that difficult to finally contact her. All it took was a letter addressed to the street address of the place with his cellular telephone number. Brady decided after the first barrage of cussing that he probably had LaRhonda on the other end of the line.

She finally calmed down. "Your father is only concerned about your welfare. If you are tied up with a cult you could be in danger."

"We're not a cult. It's not like the media portrays us. We're just people trying to prepare for bad times. Don't you listen to and see the news every day? It's just a matter of time before we have a nuclear war, bio-chemical war, or something."

Brady watched the voice stress analyzer as she talked. All indications were that she was telling the truth. He trusted his judgment as much as he did the voice stress analyzer. He believed her.

"I'd like to come out there and meet with you, with your friends around you. If I'm convinced you are okay, I'll tell your father as much."

"You're willing to come out here by yourself? What if we are what you say?"

"Then I'll be right and you lied to me. I believe you, but I owe it to your father to confirm it in person."

"Hang on."

Brady could hear discussion going on in the background. LaRhonda came back onto the line and said, "Sam says it is okay. But be warned, they won't let you take me away, even if you have help."

"I'm not going to try to take you away, based on what you've said."

"Okay. Tomorrow at 2:00 PM. Someone will meet you at the gate. You'd better come by yourself."

"I will. You have my word."

After LaRhonda broke the connection Brady leaned back in the hotel chair and relaxed. He might be running into trouble tomorrow at 2:00 PM, but he was prepared to handle it.

"Prepared," he thought. "Interesting word."

CHAPTER TWO

Brady was prompt. He showed up at the gate right at 2:00 PM. Of course, he'd been parked down the road quite a ways and had scouted the compound from the cover of the forest surrounding it.

He saw six houses, a barn, large outdoor garden, an orchard, and a greenhouse, a couple other outbuildings and people working here and there. There was no sign of armed guards circulating. All the men and most of the women he saw did have holstered handguns.

"Clever," Brady thought when he noticed the blackberry bushes surrounding the compound. He wouldn't want to try to push his way through those.

The man was curt at the gate. It was the same one he'd talked to previously. He too was wearing a holstered pistol. "You Collingsworth?" At Brady's nod, he unchained the gate and swung it open. It put him on the driver's side of the Suburban.

A rather begrudging "Nice truck," passed the man's lips as Brady drove past. "Just follow the road. Someone will meet you at the compound."

There was a welcoming committee. Brady judged it to be half the population of the compound. No children. He stopped the Suburban next to a small line of vehicles. He noted that they were all older models.

"Hello," he said as he got out of the Suburban. "I'm Brady Collingsworth."

"Sam Fellows," said what was obviously the leader of the clan. He just had that look about him, to Brady.

"Excuse me if I don't shake hands." Sam crossed his arms when Brady held out his hand for a handshake.

Brady shrugged. "Can't really blame you. Am I going to be allowed to talk to LaRhonda?"

"She said she would," came a voice from the back of the small crowd. "That means she will." The voice was tinged with anger.

"Come on in to the house," Sam said. The group parted and Sam led Brady to the closest of the six houses. He had to force himself to turn his attention back to the matter at hand. The construction features of the house had caught his eye.

Brady saw LaRhonda sitting stiffly in an upholstered chair in the small living room of the house when they entered. He recognized her from the photos her father had given him. "Hello, LaRhonda," Brady said. He didn't even try to shake hands with her.

"I'm not leaving," she said, staring at him. "I'm safe here. Safer than out there. She made a vague motion, indicating the world outside the compound. "Don't you watch the news?"

"Mind if I sit down?" He didn't move until LaRhonda finally nodded. Sam silently left the room; going into what Brady figured was the kitchen. No doors opened and closed so Brady assumed Sam was hanging close, to lend a hand, if need be.

"Would you expand on that a little? Tell me not only why you want to stay, but also why you don't want to go back. I think there are several different issues here."

He almost wished he hadn't asked. Brady got LaRhonda's life history. And quite a bit of world history and especially US history. She was lucid and forceful in her speech. No signs of it being by rote, like she would have if she had been programmed. It was all by her own design. By the time she finished, Brady felt like he'd just attended a cross between an Oprah show and a seminar on preparedness.

Quietly Brady said, "I'll tell your father you are where you want to be. You aren't under any constraints and you could leave whenever you wanted. You just choose not to go back to your father's home."

LaRhonda's eyes widened. "That's it? You'll tell him to leave me alone?"

"I can't tell him that. That's his decision. But it will be a strongly voiced report that he shouldn't pursue trying to get you to go back."

"You sound honest. You aren't just telling me this to get my guard down so you can take me by force?"

"No, I'm not. You'll only be convinced after enough time passes with nothing happening. Then again, I can't say what your father will do after he gets my report. He may hire someone else to try. I would stay on my guard, if I was you."

"Oh."

"I'll keep my eyes and ears open. If he indicates to me that he will do that, I'll let you know. A letter might be too slow. Can I call?"

"I don't want to give you our phone number. You might give it to him."

Brady reeled off two of the phone numbers the compound had.

"You already have it," LaRhonda said, disappointed. "Well, I guess you can call. But it's hard to get through sometimes. Be better if you send me an e-mail. We have satellite internet service here. I'm the computer person for the group so I'm online quite a bit."

"Very good. I'll do that. I think I'd better be going. I don't want to cause any more commotion than I already have."

Sam immediately came out of the kitchen. He walked with Brady back to the Suburban. There were three men checking it out. "Nice truck," one said.

"Too bad it won't run after an EMP attack," said another.

"How's that?" Brady asked, intrigued.

"EMP will probably fry the computers. These new Suburbans are nice, but I'll take my old model," Sam said. "No computer or engine electronics to fry."

The third man spoke. "Be a sweet rig though, with a non-electronic turbo diesel. Where did you get the snorkel?"

"Came with it," Brady said. "I bought it at a government auction. It was a drug mule's border crossing vehicle."

"Sweet," said the first man. "Hope he got life."

"Actually," Brady said, rather grimly, "He got death. Tried to fight it out with the Border Patrol."

Brady started to get into the Suburban, but hesitated, one foot still on the ground. "Any chance, under the circumstances, of getting a tour of the place? I'm curious about…"

"No way," chorused the three men.

Sam was shaking his head. "We keep to ourselves. Visitors aren't all that welcome. And we don't give away our secrets."

"I understand," Brady said. He climbed the rest of the way into the Suburban, buckled up, and started the engine. "Non-electronic diesel, huh?" he said softly as he backed up and turned around to leave. He saw Sam take a radio from a belt pouch and speak into it.

The man at the gate had it open already. He did do a small wave as Brady passed. Brady waved back. When he got back into Branson he contacted the Branson police and county sheriff's offices that his business was concluded and he would be leaving the area.

He decided to stay one more night and catch another show.

After he had returned to the city and given LaRhonda's father his report, he e-mailed LaRhonda with the message, "Stay on guard." Her father wasn't going to give up yet.

Brady had a high profile courier case waiting on him when he returned. While he was doing that, he had Barbara checking on engine swap specialists, on a whim. She found three and had reports on each of them when he completed the delivery and returned.

"I've been wondering all week." Barbara handed Brady the files. "Is something wrong with the Suburban? I drove it this week and everything seemed all right."

"Nothing wrong," Brady replied. "Just an idea prompted by the research on the cult case." He started to turn away, but stopped and asked Barbara. "You're always on the ball. What do you do when the power goes out?"

"Oh, I've got plenty of candles. Why? You thinking about becoming a survivalist?"

Brady grinned. "Definitely not one like the media portrays them."

"Of course not. But I've heard you say you don't keep much in the fridge, much less the pantry. You eat out all the time. What would you do if the power went out? Or the stores ran out of food?"

Brady realized she was quite serious. She'd never broached the subject with him before. "I don't really know," he said slowly, staring off into the distance.

"You should think about it," Barbara replied. "Just listen to the news."

"LaRhonda said essentially the same thing." Brady's eyes refocused on Barbara. "Are you a survivalist?" When Barbara looked a little sour, Brady added, "Or whatever the term is for people that prepare, but aren't wackos?"

"Preppers. That's what I consider myself—someone who prepares for the worst, but hopes for the best."

"Prepper, huh? That does sound better. I'll give it some thought." And he did. A lot of thought. When he wasn't actively working on a case he continued the research he'd started doing during LaRhonda's case. He found the more he learned, the more he wanted to learn. He was a good detective. He learned much.

Brady began to watch the news with a different eye. He also looked for alternate sources of news. He began visiting several preparedness related websites and forums, including those that FEMA sponsored.

Then one day one of the real estate agents he'd contacted in and around Branson called him. She had found a piece of property in which he might be interested. Brady didn't tell her he was no longer in the market. He decided on the spur of the moment to go look at it.

CHAPTER THREE

The real estate agent rode with Brady. It was a hot, muggy day. Brady had the air conditioner full on. Julia directed Brady down the state road for just a short way, and then onto a county road. Soon Brady noted they were climbing in altitude. The road twisted and turned quite a bit. They'd gone almost twenty miles on the road. Brady figured it was less than fifteen as the crow flies back to Branson when Julia indicated a steep dirt track.

He turned onto it and they climbed the sharp grade. The road finally leveled off and then quickly petered out. It was forest all around, except for the dirt road. Brady had to jockey the Suburban around some in the trees to get it turned around to head back down the track.

Brady and Julia got out of the Suburban. Julia handed Brady a topographical map. "Here is the map you requested. We're… right here." She put her finger on a point on the map after Brady unfolded it.

They couldn't see more than twenty or thirty yards in any direction, except down the road, so Brady began walking along, map in hand. Julia stayed where she was. Brady had spotted key points on the map and checked each one out in person. He was trying not to grin when he returned to the Suburban and Julia. It was everything he'd asked for and Julia had told him about. Plus.

All the real estate agents had said that properties with water sources were rare and costly. They did exist, but most of them had been bought up years before, by the earliest settlers, and seldom came onto the market.

What Julia had missed on the map, if she had even looked at it, was a tiny blue mark. Barely more than a tic. It was a spring. A very small one, but a spring never-the-less. He'd been tempted to check how it tasted, but remembered in time that he'd read that even in remote areas the water was often contaminated. He'd have the water tested professionally before he tried to drink any of it.

He didn't mention the spring to Julia. He did ask, "How did this piece of property come to be on the market?"

"A group of doctors had bought it, intending to put in a small spa resort. They bought the property three years ago, based on some very tentative county plans to extend and improve the roads up here. That project fell through. They decided to cut their losses while they could. They are quite eager to sell." Julia quoted a price.

"Doesn't sound too eager to me." He made a counter, and she re-countered. Brady made his do or die offer.

"I… I'll have to check with them," Julia said. "I just don't know. I've gone as low as they would let me."

Brady shrugged. "It's a take it or leave it offer. And it will be cash. See if that makes any difference to them.

Julia looked delighted. "Oh, I think it will. Can't make promises, but I think they'll take it. They were grumbling about having to finance it."

When Brady dropped Julia off at her office he said, "If they accept the offer, push the paperwork through as fast as you can. I'd like to take possession as soon as possible."

"Are you planning a resort, too, Mr. Collingsworth?"

"No," Brady replied. "A retirement home." He suddenly realized he meant it.

After he dropped Julia off, Brady went to a hardware store and picked up a few things and then went back up to the property. He dug out the wet spot that was the source of the spring and made a small pool. He scooped up water in three zip-lock bags to take back to the city for testing.

He filled half-way full four 5-gallon plastic buckets with topsoil from four different spots on the property. Then he dug down in another spot as deep as he could without making a huge hole and put a sample of the sub-soil in another bucket. He'd take them all in for testing by the county extension service.

A week after Brady got home Julia called. The doctor group had accepted the offer. Brady overnighted a cashier's check that afternoon.

A few days later and he received the results of the water and soil tests. The water was contaminated with protozoa, but any decent silver impregnated filter would handle that.

The soil tests were also less than perfect, but more than acceptable. The soil was more than moderately fertile, but not up to intensive gardening without conditioning. He would need to do a percolation test to determine the size and type of septic system that would be needed. But he needed to decide what facilities he would have on the property before he sized the septic system.

One piece of information the real estate agents had provided him, on their own, was how deep wells in the area ran and the names of a couple of well drillers. Water was a big issue in the area.

Brady got on line and found a site with aerial photographs. He pinpointed his property. The photo was over ten years old, but perhaps for individual trees that might have died and fallen, and new growth, he couldn't see where anything else had changed.

A visit to the USGS website got him different scale topographic maps of the area. He took the maps and copies of the photos to a professional model maker he'd used on a case, and had large scale models of the property and the surrounding area built.

He began reading the Branson newspaper on line to become more familiar with the area.

His detective business was booming and he expanded during the fall, hiring two operatives in addition to Harry, one male and one female. Barbara had her license and had handled tasks for him that required a female. But she was pregnant now and wanted to just run the office.

They really needed more room for what they had, and would need even more as they expanded. "Barbara," Brady said one day, "use your detective skills and see if you can find us a decent place in a building with some kind of reasonable shelter space in case of bad weather or something."

"You a convert, Boss?" she asked in reply.

"I don't know, Barbara. I think just maybe I am. I've been thinking about it quite a bit."

He told her about the property he'd bought and she laughed. "Yep. A convert. Seriously now, if I can help you in any way, let me know. And if you would, keep me and Robert in mind if you want to start a MAG. I'd like to find a better retreat than we have, if you'd consider it."

"I'll consider it. I hadn't thought that far ahead. I still need to get a well drilled, but I can't do that until I decide where I want the house and cut some trees. You can barely move around up there right now. A drilling rig would never make it."

"Think southern exposure and defensibility, both in placement and orientation."

It was good advice. Brady kept both in mind as he continued to study the maps and the models, and plans for everything from a one room cabin on up. He had a clean slate. He could do anything he could dream up and afford. He had to put preps on a back burner for a while. The firm picked up a murder case from one of the several attorneys he was on retainer to for case investigation work. It took him out of town for quite a while. When he returned the attorney's client was set free with the actual murderer in jail, with enough evidence provided by Brady to convict him.

It had been a tough case, and dangerous. The killer had carefully set up the accused, with an alibi for himself. He didn't like it when Brady began to poke holes in the frame and the alibi. Brady set himself up as an easy target, and with police backup, trapped the guy. At least this one had enough sense not to try to shoot it out.

So Brady decided to take a couple of weeks off and go down to the property. He was born and bred a city boy. He'd been in the service, but other than boot camp hadn't gone into the field. He did his tour working for the JAG as an investigator.

He used the information from forum discussions to select camping equipment so he could stay on the property when he went down. Barbara put in her dollar and a quarter's worth and he was set. Barbara also made sure he understood the BOB concept. She nodded her approval when Brady showed her what he had come up with.

Barbara would be in charge of the move to their new offices while Brady was gone. He hated moving. The building had a sub-basement and parking garage suitable for shelter use. Between them Brady and Barbara came up with a budget to have preparations purchased and stored in the offices and sub-basement after the move.

Brady had talked to both of the available well drillers previously. One sounded fine, but the other guaranteed a minimum quantity of water if he could douse the property and put the well where he wanted. Brady had grave doubts about dousing, but the guarantee couldn't be beat, even though the driller was a dollar higher a foot than the other guy. But he wouldn't guarantee quality of the water when Brady asked about it, just the quantity.

So Brady met the driller at the property the first day Brady was down. Brady showed Henry the area where he planned for the house and compound. He watched Henry as he walked the area, two L-shaped pieces of coat hanger in his hands. Brady saw them cross or almost cross several times. Henry kept coming back to one place. "Here," he said, looking up at Brady.

It wasn't quite where Brady would have picked, but it wasn't that far off. And it was uphill from where he tentatively planned to put the septic system. It would do. Brady would get the guarantee. Henry showed Brady how much space he would need for the drilling rig and support truck.

They set a date for Henry to come back with his rig to drill the well and set the pumps. Brady had selected a solar pump as the primary pump, with a deep-well hand pump as back-up. He was taking his preps seriously.

But first he had to get the trees cleared. Firewood was a big business in the area, so it was no problem to find someone to cut the trees for a portion of the firewood. He'd stockpile the rest. Wood burning stoves were in his future.

A local farmer advertised stump removal. Brady contacted him and had him come out and dynamite the stumps. That called for some earthmoving afterwards to fill the holes and level the ground. Brady had gone undercover on a case two years previously as an equipment operator. He had more than a passing familiarity with earthmoving equipment. He just needed to decide if he wanted to rent equipment and do the work, or hire the work done.

After checking on the availability of equipment he just hired a contractor and had him do the work. Later he would do some of the work himself when he had more time. Henry was happy with the pad created and set up and got right to work when he arrived the day after the dirt work was done.

Curious, Brady monitored the operation, watching with interest as Henry worked the rig controls like a musician playing an instrument. It took most of two days of drilling to hit the best aquifer. Brady had to pay up. The well produced eleven gallons a minute, plenty for Brady's needs.

Henry was experienced with solar pumps and had everything needed to erect a fold-over pole with the solar array on it, and the controller and batteries for backup. Brady would do something else later, but Henry had a tip-up, insulated enclosure to cover the well head in the meantime. Samples of the water were sent in for tests.

Brady found he liked camping out and stayed two extra days beyond what he originally planned to just enjoy being on the property. Before he left, Brady set up a motion activated surveillance camera just inside the tree line, aimed at the well site and camouflaged it. On the off chance someone discovered the well, pump, and solar array and vandalized or stole it, he'd have proof of it and probably the identity of the perpetrators. He had digital pictures of the installation for insurance purposes and would acquire coverage for the property when he got back to the city.

He knew the next thing he needed to do was decide on the location of buildings and the number of people for which he needed to provide sewage treatment. But the work load was picking up and Brady put the decisions off for a few days. Barbara was looking for additional operatives. If he could get them, he had a big security contract in the bag and would branch out into that field.

Barbara came through, as he knew she would and Brady took a team to the new business building under construction for which he would be providing security. The original architects had included security features, but Brady suggested a few changes. The owners weren't too happy, but some of the changes actually saved some money. Overall, the changes resulted in only being slightly more expensive than the original plans. The owners were happy and Brady was happy. It would look good for advertising his services.

Brady took another two weeks off and went back down to the property. He got the same wood cutters, powder monkey, and earthmoving contractor he'd used before to clear the area where he'd decided to put the septic system. He'd studied up on various waste treatment systems and knew what he wanted. It was a basic septic tank with leach field system.

The plumbing contractor that he hired continued to tell Brady that the multi-trunk leach field was way over capacity for the tank capacity, according to the percolation test that had been done. Even for the larger than normal septic tank Brady had ordered.

But Brady stood firm and the man installed it the way Brady wanted it. Brady had learned that you could clean out a tank, but could not effectively clean a leach field if it ever became saturated.

He wanted the extra capacity for that reason and to allow for reduced evaporation in cases of extreme winter weather. In a properly installed leach field much of the liquid migrated upward through the ground, to be used by the plant life over the field, with another portion evaporating into the air. A significant amount was absorbed by the ground, but far from all of it, as most people thought, including some plumbers.

So Brady now had two of the most important basics on the property. Water and sewer. And the water had tested out pure and relatively soft. It wouldn't need any treatment and tasted good.

That was Brady's last trip for a while. Winter set in and work demands kept Brady busy. But he wasn't neglecting his new hobby. Preparedness. He was learning more and more, and buying preparations based on what he learned. Barbara had made sure the office was ready as it could be for whatever might come, be it natural or human caused. Brady approved everything and learned much from her examples.

Over the winter, in the spare time he did have, Brady began to play with building designs and their placement on the model. By springtime, he had the basic plan for the entire property modeled out.

He also took the advice of the gentleman at LaRhonda's compound and had an engine swap done to the Suburban, as well as a few more modifications to make it a better 'prepper's' rig.

CHAPTER FOUR

The first chance he had, Brady went down, brought out the wood cutters, powder monkey, and the earthmovers again and cleared the rest of the areas he needed cleared to continue with his plans.

One of the cleared areas was for a pond. It was just downhill from the spring. Brady talked to the extension agent and got the dimensions that would be acceptable for the less-than-a-gallon-a-minute spring to keep fresh. It wasn't as large as Brady hoped for, but he wanted a live pond, not a dead one. He used a polymer liner, on top of a bentonite clay layer to insure the pond wouldn't leak. The top soil was stockpiled separately from the sub-soil, for use later in building and landscaping.

Near the pond, a freshly cleared and leveled area would be the orchard. Fortunately, the forest that had covered the property included several black walnut trees and uncounted hickory trees. All seemed to be heavy producers. A local nursery brought out the largest fruit and nut trees they had in stock to populate the orchard. It would be at least two to three years before the new trees began bearing, but Brady considered the expense of the more mature trees worth it, compared to less mature trees that would take five to seven years to produce.

Three acres were cleared for gardens. Brady made arrangements with several local farms, as he located them, to either buy manure and used straw, or receive it for free to haul it off. It would all go on the garden plots for a couple of years to enrich the soil before anything was planted. One of the farmers was willing to go around, collect it, and deposit it on the garden for a small monthly fee. Brady also contracted with him to seed the pasture area that had been cleared.

Brady also had large beds of ever bearing strawberries put in, and blackberries, the thorny type. Brady had sets placed all around the perimeters of each of the cleared areas. More would be added each year until he had a solid ring around each area, except for specific, necessary openings.

That was the springtime project. The summer project began in July.

Brady bought another solar pump setup identical to the one for the well. It was placed in the pond and a line run to the garden and one to the orchard. The nursery crew came back out and installed an irrigation system in the orchard. A drip system fed perforated pipes that went down to the roots of each tree. The drips were adjusted to provide each tree with an optimum amount of water supplied from the solar pump in the pond. The pump had float switches wired into the controls so it wouldn't pump the pond completely dry.

He brought a local concrete construction contractor in and had a one-hundred-thousand-gallon underground water tank constructed. It was designed with enough support columns inside to allow a twelve inch concrete roof covered with three feet of earth, and still allow heavy equipment to travel over it.

A month later he brought in a contractor from some distance away to put in a second "water tank" using the same construction techniques. Brady ran a line to the first tank from the well pump and began filling it with water. The second he didn't. When it was finished, it would be a 30' x 45' x 9' blast, fallout, and environmental shelter with two entrance/exits and an escape tunnel. But the final work would be done by someone he trusted with the information.

While they were there on the second tank project, Brady had one of the mason's chip out the rock around the spring opening. It wound up increasing the flow to just over a gallon a minute, though that wasn't why Brady wanted it done. Brady wanted a moderate sized spring house built flush to the ground for actual use, but primarily to protect the spring from surface contamination. A pipe, buried deep to avoid freezing, was run down to the pond. They left a way for the water to escape the spring house on the surface, just in case the pipe did freeze or become blocked. It wasn't good to put back pressure on a spring.

The final project for the summer, into fall, was installing the heat sink piping for a geothermal, ground source, heating, ventilation, air conditioning (HVAC) system. It so happened that bigger was better, so Brady used 30" inside diameter clay tiles for the system. He marked out where he wanted the tiles to go. A second contractor put in more of the tiles. Both were told they were being put in now, but the system wouldn't be completed until he was ready to build. He wanted to be able to landscape the area and not disturb it later, except for digging up the ends and making connections.

Since the contractors dug where Brady marked, they had no idea one of the strings of tiles stopped just short of the second "water tank", with others conveniently placed where they would be adjacent to the buildings Brady would have erected. Some of them were actually for the HVAC system.

Brady put up a few more cameras with recorders around the perimeter of the main area. He drove down at least once a month during the winter to check the DVDs and change the batteries for freshly charged ones. All that ever showed up on the recordings was wild life, a great deal of it, and the occasional hunter passing through. None had done anything to the well, pumps, or pond, which were about the only things showing above ground.

The next spring Brady had the first structure on the property built. It was a large utility room and garage, built over a half basement with the well a ways inside one end wall. The foundations were substantial, including the basement walls. The building walls consisted of an outer wall of reinforced, grout-filled, concrete block.

Inside the block wall solid foam insulation was sprayed on, and then a twelve inch thick, staggered six inch stud, wood wall was erected, covered on the living space with ¾" marine plywood and vapor barrier, and the space between the plywood and insulated block wall filled with minus ¾" crushed rock. A six-inch concrete ceiling was poured and then an enameled steel hipped roof installed over it, a thick layer of insulation being sprayed in to cover the ceiling.

The openings for several small windows, three regular doors, and three 9' garage doors were left empty. The doors and windows would be installed later. Two cameras went into the building. There still wasn't much to steal, just the pumps. The building might be vandalized, but Brady was prepared for that. Even the steps down to the basement area of the building were of steel, not subject to much damage.

He did the same with the electrical and plumbing. The rough-ins were done, but the finish components were not installed.

Then Brady had some walls constructed, sort of here and there, going all different directions. He made tall, thick walls with deep foundations, some of them quite long. The walls were reinforced concrete block on one side and the ends, and interlocking retaining wall blocks on the other. The two rows of blocks were tied together regularly with metal ties. The area between the block walls was filled with compacted crushed rock, five feet wide at the top, seven at the bottom. Two of the walls connected to the garage/utility building, but were freestanding on the other ends.

The walls took everything he had budgeted for the year, and then some. He got a couple of complaints from the gravel pit operators from which he was sourcing the rock. He was taking everything they were producing and his other regular customers were complaining.

But the business was booming. He and Harry, plus two others, concentrated on the detective work. Barbara was running the security operation and had hired two office staff to help her.

The following year Brady didn't do any building. Instead he made occasional trips to camp out, change batteries on the surveillance equipment, and check on the place. And empty the heavily laden Suburban of its contents to put them into the shelter space through one of the roof hatches each trip. He carefully covered the hatch up each time and camouflaged it before he left.

So far, the civilization had not ended and Brady had spent a small fortune already to prepare for it. That didn't deter Brady. All the things he was seeing happening here in the good ol' USA, as well as events around the world, had him convinced that it was only a matter of when, not if, he would need to use his major preparations. He'd already used the minor ones. He'd been stuck on the highway twice, for hours each time. St. Louis had another flood, and this winter was shaping up to be a record breaker. Nothing that made him want to leave the city. Yet. He took comfort in the knowledge that he could, now.

All through the process over the years that had passed, beside learning and acquiring things, and building, Brady had been cultivating people. Very carefully. Many of those he was feeling out were his employees, but by no means were they the majority.

Barbara was a given. She had a place for her family reserved at Brady's. And since the apartment where he lived wasn't really prep friendly, she reciprocated with offering her house for local bug-in situations for him.

He'd found out the hard way, despite Barbara's admonishment to be careful, that selling the idea of preps was a hard job and needed just the right touch. And then it didn't always work. He lost one of his few friends when he began insisting that he and his family become more prepared.

Brady was much more careful after that. And since he didn't really consider himself as expert at preparedness, since he'd only been preparing such a short time, he began trying to get people to visit some of the websites where he'd learned so much. That was in addition to the FEMA sponsored sites, which seemed to elicit a better response.

But as things worsened in the world, some of the people were becoming more open to the idea of preparing. He began to get the makings of a mutual aid group, or MAG. Barbara was a big help in that. She'd been working toward it for years. Just hadn't found the right people. But Brady was good with people for the most part.

Barbara, Harry, and three other employees finally committed to building on Brady's property, and contributing, to one degree or another, to some of the projects Brady wanted to do. He really wanted three more major investors, though two would allow him to complete the project the way he had come to envision it.

Both Jonesy and Lieutenant Sandra Harrison bought in as minor investors.

Even a couple of the major news networks were hinting at the possibility of one of the regional wars expanding to a new World War. Global warming was a fact, and its effects were beginning to affect the world's weather and coastlines.

Finally Brady's doctor saw the handwriting on the wall. Dr. Amos was one of the people Brady had been gently working on, to bring him into the fold. Dr. Amos, one dentist, and one other doctor in his practice agreed to join the MAG. All three would build at the compound and invest in the communal projects.

About the time that Harry took three rounds of .380 ACP in a shootout with gang members he was tracking, Brady got the surprise of his life. A national security firm wanted to buy his operation. It had a very good reputation and was still growing. They wanted in on that growth.

Brady negotiated with the company's representatives for a month and got the price up considerably more than their first offer, and most importantly, got an immediate buy out, rather than the term buyout the company wanted. Brady was able to stay on as a very well paid consultant and contract operative.

It turned him loose to get started on the rest of the building he would be supervising. Harry agreed to move to the compound with his family and keep an eye on the place during the construction of his own place, as well as Brady's place and the construction of the community features. He was recovering well, but it would take some months before he was ready for action again. He was able to get around enough to supervise the contractors.

Brady already knew the contractor he would use to build his house and had the drawings ready. The others were free to hire pretty much whomever they wanted. There were a few stipulations in the agreement Brady had with the others. One was that each of the houses had to be built between the existing freestanding walls.

Another was that the housing unit have a back wall built similar to the existing walls, with both block walls being reinforced concrete block. And that wall had to be placed so it projected five feet beyond the existing walls, parallel to them, with a slight bend at the center. That would give defensive coverage along each of the walls from the side.

A third was that the unit must have a full height, full basement, designed with fallout protection in mind for at least one fourth of it, with another fourth set aside for prep storage.

The unit had to be energy efficient and set up to go totally off grid when necessary. Brady left it open for the owners to choose their own power and fuel sources. All fuel tanks would be located together in an area protected by berms. Brady had allowed enough space for his own tanks, the community tanks, and the private tanks to be installed.

Getting the fuel tanks installed and bermed was the first thing Brady did after he had the commitments he wanted. That and getting them filled. He footed the bill to fill the private tanks so they would be full come what may. Everyone was beginning to feel a sense of urgency. Plans for the individual housing units were finalized within two months.

Brady was able to contract to have all the basements dug at the same time, gravel drains put in, with the drains and basement sumps piped to the pond. The basement walls were poured and back filled before winter set in. Long lead items were ordered. Construction would start as soon as reasonably good weather in the spring arrived. Everyone hoped they would be allowed the time.

Others seemed to be getting concerned enough to begin making preparations, like the majority of Brady's MAG that hadn't been prepping for some time. They were getting put on back order lists for many of the items on the recommended equipment and supplies list that Brady and Barbara had developed for the MAG.

Brady's chosen contractor began work on his housing unit in March, as did Harry's, after a very mild winter in the area. Barbara's unit was started in April, and the others in May. Except the world situation had calmed somewhat, and three of the participants were waffling on whether or not to continue in the MAG. One was a primary investor, the other two minor.

Not wanting anyone involved that wasn't completely dedicated, he refunded most of their money, excepting the expenses he'd already expended on their behalf. Brady went ahead and began construction of the unit the primary participant that had opted out was going to do. He also brought in two additional contractors to begin building the common buildings.

Brady was only taking selected cases with the national firm so he was able to spend much of his time overseeing the construction, with Harry's help. Harry had brought in a fifth-wheel travel trailer for him and his wife to live in during the construction phase. Brady just camped out while he was there.

But then Brady was called in for a big insurance case. He had to go under cover. The case took three months to break. During that entire time Brady refused to break cover, trusting Harry and Barbara to handle anything that came up at the compound. The case involved a substantial reward, which the company split with Brady. More money for preps, he decided. It all went into gold and silver coins.

When he finally got back to the compound he was impressed and pleased with the progress. Both his and Harry's units were constructed, though not finished inside. Barbara's was close, and the others were coming along nicely, as were the common buildings.

With the additional money from the buyout, Brady had started negotiations to get commercial power to the site. They had stalled, but during the three months Brady was gone Barbara had continued to pester the power company. They finally agreed to split the cost with the MAG of bringing in the new line from the nearest source.

The line would be pole mounted until it reached the compound. From the transformer bank at the edge of the main clearing the service lines would go underground. Brady had to do some tricky trench design work to get the main line into the compound perimeter to avoid the various tunnels.

Like he had done with co-workers and acquaintances in St. Louis, Brady had begun building up friendships within and around Branson. That included the Branson police and the county sheriff and his deputies. They introduced him to the Missouri Highway Patrolmen that worked the area.

They were well aware of the several survivalist compounds in the area. So far none had developed into the media description of survivalists, but they were keeping a wary eye on all of them they knew about.

Brady was fairly open with them all about what he was doing, without revealing too much. They seemed to appreciate his coming to them openly about the compound. It helped that he lent his talents to them on a couple of cases on an informal basis.

One of the Branson officers, as well as one of the sheriff's deputies, contacted Brady and expressed an interest in joining the MAG. Brady was happy to invite them in as minor investors. He was relatively certain that each of them would keep their respective departments apprised of the goings-on of the MAG, but Brady was keeping it strictly legal, and decided the advantages outweighed the disadvantages.

Another was the farmer that was bringing in the manure for the garden plot. Brady convinced him to join the MAG as a no dollar investment outside member. The farmer would be responsible for the garden plot and orchard. His own farm would provide beef, chicken, pork, and dairy products at a reduced, guaranteed, price, for a spot in the compound for him and his family.

The MAG would finance some shelter space on site at the farm, and help provide security if it ever became necessary. It would also subsidize a fuel alcohol still and a small scale biodiesel production set up if the farmer would put some of his fields into good oil producing plants.

As the gaps between the existing walls became filled with the housing units the compound became a real compound. It was going into winter before all the housing units were completed. All the primary investors had used the same construction method as had Brady in his construction of the garage/utility building, creating fire and bullet resistant walls, even inside the compound.

Though the political situations around the world were still calm, Brady continued with the preparations, despite the winter coming on. He hoped for a mild winter like the one previous, but he didn't count on it. It was well he didn't. The final touches on three commercial green houses in the middle of the compound were completed in a light snowfall.

More of the solar water pumps were paralleled in the concrete water tank, and fed to a thousand gallon pressure tank to provide the pressurized well water to all the buildings.

Two of the manufactured housing units Brady had ordered got stuck on the road coming in during a heavy rain. They wouldn't be placed until the following spring, when they could be retrieved without damaging them.

The manufactured housing units were for the minor investors. Well insulated and efficient, they offered little ballistic and only moderate fire protection. The residents would use the community shelter if it became necessary. The units that made it were placed against the inside compound walls.

Two of the units were set up as dorms, each with a kitchen. One for men and one for women, for those single persons that were part of the MAG. The rest were single family housing units. The commercial power line was installed, and service lines connected to all the buildings.

Brady had substantially more housing availability than he did members of the MAG, but had wanted the extra for the probable late joiners he fully expected when things became really bad.

They certainly weren't bad that late winter of 2008. The Summer Olympic Games had gone off without a hitch and China was the new darling boy on the block. The Chinese leadership had calmed down North Korea and supposedly put a stop to their nuclear weapons arsenal acquisitions. They had also backed off their rhetoric about Taiwan.

Even the Middle East was in cooperative mood, with half a dozen different peace talks going on among the various Arab/Muslim countries and Israel. The US's only presence in Iraq now was their new embassy compound. The Sunni – Shi'ite internecine warfare was being kept low key. Gold prices began to drop, as did oil prices.

Brady lost another major investor and three minor ones. He bought out their equity and began looking for more people, concentrating on the local population. He didn't find any. People were saying a true peace across the globe was in the works. Of course, that didn't affect natural disasters. But even those had slowed down, the planet seeming to be in a resting state. At least that was the way Brady saw it. And he didn't trust the final World Peace talk. He continued his personal preps.

It continued that way into 2010, then, as they say, balloons started going up all over. Heavy blizzard from Montana, North Dakota, and the UP of Michigan all the way down into Iowa, Nebraska, and Wyoming.

The Yellowstone Caldera began acting up. Mt. Vesuvius had a major eruption. China and Russia cancelled a scheduled joint military exercise, with harsh words for each other. Two of the new Republics went communist again. North Korea did another nuke test and a long range missile test within days of each other. China marshaled forces on the coast opposite Taiwan, when Taiwan began talking about an independence initiative. California had yet another major earthquake.

Oil prices jumped. Gold prices jumped. Former members of the MAG jumped to get back in. Brady let them, at full price, cash on the barrelhead. Two more of his ex-employees joined the MAG as minor investors. Three of the employees of the various contractors that had worked on the site joined. One as a major investor, two as minor.

Another local farmer, retired, wanted in. He and his family were welcomed. They would be the MAG greenhouse supervisors, as well as take care of the farm animal population when the animals were purchased. Brady had wanted some on-site production in addition to the agreement with the other farmer. Other members of the MAG would help.

Brady brought in another concrete contractor and added five foot high, two foot thick, crenellated parapet walls on top of the existing walls and buildings that comprised the compound building perimeter. The place suddenly took on the look of a rather short castle. But it was finished.

After contacting everyone in the MAG, they arranged a test run, with all but two people able to schedule a trip to the site. Both of those people had been there during the building process and knew the way.

The final purchases that Brady had made came in well before the first day of the test run. It was the community vehicles and equipment for gardening and maintenance. With the equipment on hand the contractors that were part of the MAG made the final connections of the tunnels to the various buildings. And exterior entrances were made for the 'water tank' blast shelter to use instead of the original access hatches.

Brady welcomed everyone and gave a tour of the place as people began arriving the first day of the test run. Several of the MAG members were unaware of the extent of the community aspects of the retreat. Most were pleased. A tiny handful were vocal about where their money was spent. Brady offered to buy them out. All refused and let it go.

It was the first time many of the MAG members had met. Brady made it obvious that he was in overall charge, and final arbitrator of all disputes. But he encouraged them to get together, get to know one another, and work out the group dynamics of who would be in charge of what aspect of the community, and set up a division of labor for the various community tasks.

One of the first tasks set up for that first day of the two day event was to organize an inspection and approval of everyone's MAG required equipment and supplies. There was a wide disparity in preparedness states. Several people were encouraged to upgrade what they already had. More than a few were congratulated on their state of preparedness. No one was asked to reveal their entire preparations, only the MAG mandated ones.

Everyone left with a better understanding of what the retreat provided them and their responsibility to it and the MAG, beside the monetary aspect of it. The second farmer and his wife decided to take up permanent residence. That would allow the acquisition of the farm animals. Two of the minor investors were college students and agreed to stay and help during the summer school break for just a small salary.

Harry was recovered and ready to go back to the agency, but his wife didn't want him to go back. She was afraid he might be killed. So Harry took a dispatching job with the county and he and his wife and first child also took up permanent residency. Brady was satisfied that the place would be well looked after while he continued to work.

CHAPTER FIVE

Brady worked for the corporation until late in 2010, when his two-year contract was up. He didn't renew it. The company was giving him basic cases, using salaried agents to work the more lucrative insurance recovery cases that Brady was so good at solving.

He continued to work, mostly as a courier, respecting the non-competition agreement he'd signed for the company. Brady had specifically exempted courier work from the agreement, along with a couple of other lines of work that he enjoyed that wouldn't really impact the company if he was on the playing field.

It was on the return trip into St. Louis after a New York to LA courier delivery that Brady heard the news about Taiwan. The Captain of the aircraft announced it. The sitting Taiwanese government had passed a resolution to call a constitutional congress as the first step to Independence. China had begun to attack the near coast of Taiwan, in preparation to invade.

Brady didn't quite hold his breath until they landed, but he would have if he could have. He felt much better when he was sitting in the Suburban, armed again. He listened to the news as he drove toward his apartment.

His landline was ringing when he arrived at the apartment. It was Barbara, asking him if he'd heard the news.

"Yeah. On the plane."

"We're bugging out first thing in the morning," Barbara told him. "What about you?"

"Maybe. I want to see how this begins to track out. I have another job I'm supposed to start Monday."

"You hear the weather forecast?"

"No. I haven't. Why?"

"An arctic front is headed this way. They're predicting a foot of snow accumulation here by Saturday morning. Freezing rain twenty miles north and south of an east west line through Poplar Bluff. You know what ice storms do to that country."

"Yeah. Look. I just don't know. I think you're smart to leave tomorrow. Don't be surprised if you see me in your rearview mirror. But don't count on it, either."

"You take care, Brady. Don't wait too long, if this Taiwan situation gets worse. I know you are a dedicated worker, even independently, but don't let it get you killed."

"I won't. Promise. I gotta go. Just in case, I'm going to go fuel up the Suburban. It's down to three-quarters."

"Shame. Shame. 'Bye."

Brady hung up the phone and went back to the parking garage. It took him a good half an hour to get to the local station and fill the Suburban's tanks with diesel. He kept the radio on to listen to the news.

The US government had issued a strong protest and called a UN Security Council session. Two carrier groups were ordered to sail at full steam to the area. China was warning off all nations to stay out of its local affairs. Taiwan was part of China and would remain so.

Brady stayed up late, watching the news. All the news networks had it as lead and secondary stories. Brady knew nothing would be resolved that night. He made sure his

SAME NOAA NWS radio had fresh batteries in it. He put it on the nightstand beside his bed.

No alarm sounded during the night. Brady got up the next morning and went out for breakfast. At nine o'clock sharp he called the client he was to work for the following Monday. It was now Thursday morning. He talked the client into letting him pick up the package that afternoon for delivery Friday afternoon. The client didn't like it, but Brady didn't leave him much choice.

He had worked for him before and was not too impressed with his business or his interpersonal skills. Had he known what the package was this time, he would have turned down the job. Previously it had always been small, extremely expensive museum quality art objects going to private collectors. Brady had checked the man out and there were no indications of illegal activities, but Brady always felt greasy after dealing with him.

When he arrived at the man's studio, he immediately smelled a rat. Parkinson was waiting for him, a frown on his face. Sitting casually in a chair nearby was a woman, dressed in red. Brady took a second look. She smiled a friendly smile at him and he had to smile in return.

"Let's go into my office," Parkinson said, leading the way. "Normally I don't like to be rushed," he said as soon as the door closed behind Brady. "But you may have a point. The weather could delay you if you wait to leave Monday. And I promised delivery by Wednesday of next week in Kansas City."

"At least it isn't across the country the way it usually was, just across the state," Brady thought. "What's the package this time?"

Brady didn't like the way Parkinson hesitated and shifted his eyes. "You know I won't do anything illegal."

"It's not illegal," Parkinson quickly said. "It's just sort of unusual," Parkinson hesitated again, and then said, "You saw the woman out there? It's her."

"Her? Are you joking?" Brady was incensed. He turned around when the door opened behind him.

"You tell him about me?" asked the woman in red. She moved to stand at the end of Parkinson's desk, staring inquisitively at Brady.

"Sort of. Just that you were the package."

"You look like a big girl," Brady said. "I doubt you need a baby sitter on a trip to KC."

"Actually I'm only a B-cup," she said, taking Brady totally by surprise at her announcement. "And Daddy says I need a keeper, not a baby sitter."

"I'm not getting involved in some kind of kidnapping situation," Brady said, thinking suddenly of LaRhonda.

"It's not kidnapping," Parkinson immediately said.

"Then what's the problem of her getting on a plane or a bus and heading out on her own?"

Parkinson as much as wrung his hands in misery. "It's complicated."

"Money," Red said. "I don't have any. Spent every last dime Daddy put in the credit card account. He won't let me use American Express."

"So have him wire you some. Or get Parkinson here to spring for the ticket."

"Don't want to. Want Daddy to pay for it. He won't."

"Look, Collingsworth… Cut me a break, will you? He one of my biggest customers." He glared at Red. She just grinned at him. "And she knows it. She won't go home unless I hire a bodyguard, and turn around and charge her father for it."

"You knew about this a week ago and don't already have it sorted out?" Brady asked, more than a little annoyed.

"I can be difficult," Red said, again rather matter-of-factly. "Daddy always says so. So it must be true."

"I'm out of here," Brady said, rising from the chair.

Red made chicken clucking noises. Brady turned as red as Red's hair and outfit.

"Tell you what, Pretty Boy; I'll add triple to what you're getting from him, if you do it." She nodded toward Parkinson.

"You said you spent every dime. It doesn't sound like your father would fork it over when I get there," Brady replied, his annoyance growing at Red's calm demeanor.

"Actually, I'm lying."

"About what? Being out of money or paying me?"

Red grinned. "Yes."

Brady almost growled. "How old are you? You're acting like a sixteen year old."

"Why, thank you. But no. I'm legal. I'm twenty-six."

Brady couldn't help it. His mouth dropped open and his eyes widened. She sure looked a lot closer to sixteen than she did twenty-six.

It took a moment, but Brady finally responded. "No. It's ridiculous."

Red made the clucking sounds again. "Stop that," Brady said.

"Come on," she said. "It's just a game. Play it and win and you'll be rewarded."

"Wait a minute," Brady said, frowning, "why wouldn't I be successful? You said you were willing to go, just with an escort."

"Well, things just sort of happen around me. Daddy always says so."

"Lord have mercy," Parkinson said. "She's right. She's a jinx." Red stuck her tongue out at him.

That settled it for Brady. There was no way he was going to saddle himself with her, with everything going on, jinx or not. She was just too unstable. He felt his conscience twinge as he turned to leave. Red moved over to him and linked her left arm through his right. "By the way. Don't ever call me Red. I know you were thinking it," she said as they were walking out the office door.

Brady struggled just slightly, but her grip was firm. He resigned himself to the fact that he was escorting her to Kansas City. "Okay. Deal. Don't call me Pretty Boy. My name is Brady. What should I call you?"

"Daddy calls me Precious."

"I am not going to call you Precious!" Brady insisted. "What is your given name?"

"Precious."

Brady groaned.

"I know," she said then, laughing at him, "I always figured that if I ever had to be an exotic dancer to make a living if Daddy cut me off, I'd use the name Star. You can call me that."

Brady didn't respond to that directly. He asked, "Where are your bags and things."

"The hotel is holding them. I haven't paid the bill."

"Great. I'll spring for it. I'll make sure Parkinson pays me back."

"Actually, I'll send them the money when I get back home. Take my word for it, it will be cheaper on you to buy me new than to get my stuff out of hock."

"You don't really need anything else," Brady said. It's only a long day's drive."

"Actually I do," she said, leaning over toward him as if to whisper confidentially. "You see, it's that time of the month. I need the works."

Brady hung his head for a moment, and then turned on the turn signal, checked the traffic behind and moved into the left turn lane. "There's a mall just up here," he said.

"You are so sweet, Brady."

"Don't push it… Star."

Star giggled.

Brady pulled into the mall and stopped. He gave Star two hundred in twenties. "Just get what you really need. I'll wait here."

"Spoilsport," Star said. But she took the money and got out of the Suburban.

Brady saw her shiver. Then she was jogging toward the mall entrance. He turned on the news to see what was going on. It wasn't good. The local weather or the world news.

He almost didn't recognize her when Star approached the truck. Before she'd been red. Now she was blue. Blue jeans, blue shirt, blue denim jacket. What broke the color scheme was the St. Louis Cardinals baseball cap. It was red.

She opened the second seat passenger door and set three shopping bags inside, and then climbed into the front passenger seat. She handed Brady some money. He was a bit surprised there was as much as there was.

He put it away and started the Suburban. "Ready?" he asked, looking over at her.

She nodded and buckled up. Brady headed out of town, finally picking up Interstate 70 west. Before they left the suburbs Brady pulled into a Bonanza Steak House and they ordered dinner while the sun was going down. Star had a healthy appetite, Brady noticed, though she didn't gorge. She did pass on dessert, as did Brady. Then they were on the road again, the light almost gone

"Can we listen to some music?" She asked after a while.

"I really want to keep it on the news, with everything going in like it is."

"Sure," Star replied. "I don't really mind. What's going on really brings out how petty I am about this doesn't it?"

Brady glanced at her, but brought his eyes back to the road. Traffic was heavy. He didn't say anything.

"Oh, it's okay. I know how I am. I do it on purpose to get attention. Usual story, I won't bore you with it other than to tell you I love my father and he loves me despite how I have made it sound."

Star was silent for a while and then asked, "What do you think about all this stuff that is going on? Are we at real risk of war?"

"I think so," Brady said.

"It is history repeating itself. People just never seem to learn from the past," Star said with a sigh.

"That is so true," Brady said, surprised and pleased at Star's remark. "You seem to have a good grasp of history."

"I should. It was my major in college. I intended to become a teacher. Didn't work out. The career counselor recommended against it. I was too independent minded, though she didn't put it that way."

"I can see that," Brady said with a smile directed at Star. "Seems like much of the education system is more interested in teaching a politically correct agenda than having independent thinking going on."

"Don't get me started," Star replied with a snort. "So. What do you do besides escorting devilish children home?"

Brady found himself telling her all about his detective career. Star listened, keeping quiet, except for the occasional prompting question. Then Brady yawned hugely. "We're going to have to stop," He told Star. "I need some rest."

"Okay. I'm sleepy, too. I can't sleep when traveling."

It was another thirty minutes before they came to a motel with a vacancy sign on. Star followed Brady inside the office when he stopped the Suburban. Star stood nearby, looking through the tourist brochure rack while Brady arranged for the rooms. She was surprised when he came over to her so quickly.

"We'll have to try another place. They've only got one room left."

Star was eyeing another couple coming into the lobby. "Single or twin?" she quickly asked Brady.

"Twin, but…"

Star gave him a little shove to hurry him back to the desk. "Take it. I trust you."

"But…"

Star nudged him again. "Hurry, or that couple will get it."

Brady could usually think on his feet very well. He had to be able to, in his line of work. But Star affected him in some way he couldn't quite define. He stepped over to the desk before the other couple got there. "We'll take the room."

He came back over to her in a few minutes and handed her a card key. "I'll just sleep in the Suburban," he said, leading her toward the lobby doors.

"Don't be silly, Brady. We're both grown-ups here, despite my somewhat childish antics at times. You said there were twin beds. You'll just have to keep your eyes closed at certain times."

Brady was feeling fatigued. It had been a tiring job from which he'd just returned, and on top of that he'd stayed up late the previous night. He really didn't want to look for another place or sleep in the Suburban. And Star was persuasive.

"Okay. Okay. We'll share the room. Come on."

Star followed him out to the Suburban, smiling slightly. They took the Suburban to the far end of the row of two story rooms. Brady had to park it some distance from the room. Star hopped out, opened the rear passenger seat door and took out two of the three bags she'd set inside from her quick shopping trip.

"You need the other bag?" Brady asked as he got his grip out of the back of the Suburban.

"No, but thanks. It's the outfit I had on before."

Brady led the way to the second floor room. He wondered if Star was cold. All she had was the light jacket and it was starting to get cold. That front was traveling faster than first predicted.

After he set his bag down on one of the beds, Brady turned on the television while Star went to the bathroom. There was live coverage from one of the carriers bound for Taiwan. Brady watched the news while Star took her shower and prepared for bed. Though he was turned away from the bathroom door, when Star asked him through the slightly opened door to close his eyes, he did so.

His sharp ears could hear her pad to the other bed, pull back the bedspread and sheets and climb in. "Okay," she said.

Brady got up and went to the bathroom himself, taking his grip, keeping his eyes averted from the other bed. He didn't see Star smiling at him. When he came out of the bathroom several minutes later Star was laying on her side, apparently already asleep. Brady turned off the TV, slipped out of his silk robe, slid into the second bed. He fell asleep almost immediately.

He woke up at his normal time the next morning. Star was still asleep, her long red hair spread over the pillow and her face. Brady shook his head, went to the bathroom, and then went to start the Suburban. A light snow began to fall as he went back to the room.

The television was on and Star was in the bathroom when he got back. The Taiwan situation was taking a back seat this morning on the local channel. The approaching blizzard was headline news. Not only was it faster than predicted, but much stronger. Brady was frowning when Star came out of the bathroom.

"You look worried," she said, seeing the expression on his face. "China start something already?"

Brady shook his head. "No. It's the weather. That blizzard may hit before we get to KC."

"Why not just stay here until it blows over?" Star asked. "Seriously. I'll see that Daddy reimburses you for the expenses."

"It's not the money," Brady said. "I just... had somewhere I wanted to be as soon as possible."

"Oh, my! I've really interfered with your plans. I'm sorry."

Brady thought she looked about to cry. "It's all right. It wasn't a rigid timeframe. Just as soon as I could. It's still the same way."

"Look. Why don't you just take off? I'll make it the rest of the way on my own," Star said, very quietly.

"Not likely. I said I would get you there and I will."

"One of those, huh?"

"I'm afraid so. The Suburban should be warm by now. We can leave as soon as you're ready."

"I'm ready." She gathered her coat tightly about her when she stepped outside. The light snow was being blown about by a strong wind, but she didn't complain about the cold. They stopped and got a fast food breakfast and then headed for Interstate 70 again.

Traffic was already flowing fairly heavily, despite the weather, much of it commercial trucking. "The goods have to move," Brady said aloud as he merged alongside one and behind another as he got on the Interstate.

"What?" Star asked.

"All the trucks. Moving goods."

"Oh. You know, I read somewhere that there is only a three day supply of food in most grocery stores. They depend on regular deliveries just to stay open."

"True," Brady said. "Sad state of affairs." The snow was getting heavier. Brady turned on the wipers. "Way too many people are dependent on those deliveries for their next meal."

"I suppose so. Since I read that I've often wondered what I would do if the trucks stopped running for some reason. Like a strike or something. Since I travel so much I don't keep much in the apartment. I eat out a lot and over at Daddy's the rest of the time."

"I used to be that way. The eating out part."

"But you're not now? Are you a survivalist?" Brady noted that she didn't use the term as a derogative one.

"Well… a prepper. To a degree," Brady responded, not willing to say much more than that, on general principles.

"I guess the term Survivalist has a lot of bad connotations now, doesn't it. Prepper sounds better."

"You've got that right. How about you?" Brady asked, taking a quick look at her and then getting his eyes back on the road. "You said you wonder about a truck strike. Have you been stocking up on food since then?"

Star sighed. "No. More of a do as I say, not as I do, person."

Brady didn't respond. He was concentrating on driving in the blowing snow and heavy traffic. Most of the big rigs had slowed down and were stacked up in the right lane. Many drivers were taking advantage of that, passing long strings of them at high speed. Brady matched his pace with the trucks and eased over into the right lane.

The wind was coming from the north and several of the semis were having trouble keeping their trucks in the right hand lane. A Ford Excursion blew past Brady on the left, but had to swerve to avoid being sideswiped.

The driver lost it and the Excursion went into the median at high speed, flipping over twice, winding up on its roof. Like all the big rigs within sight of the accident, Brady pulled over and jumped out of the Suburban, telling Star to use the OnStar button to get help. He had to jerk back to avoid another car traveling at high speed. When the way was clear he ran over to join the group of truck drivers at the Excursion.

A couple of them had fire extinguishers at the ready, with the others trying to get the doors open. Brady heard a siren in the distance. Since the others seemed to have the situation in hand and the authorities were on the way, Brady stepped back, still ready to lend a hand if needed.

One of the drivers had a window punch and starred the wind shield more than it already was. Two more stepped in and cleaned the glass out with gloved hands. Brady ran back to the Suburban and got a couple of blankets out of the back and took them back to the wreck.

The front seat passenger was being eased out of the vehicle when Brady got back. He spread out one of the blankets and the woman was placed on it. While the truck driver that had stabilized her head during the removal continued to keep her spine aligned, Brady wrapped her with the rest of the blanket. She had no obvious signs of injury, but she was out cold.

He laid out the other blanket, but those trying to get the other passengers were having difficulty. A State Trooper showed up and after evaluating the scene had everyone back away from the Excursion, except for the two fire extinguisher wielders. He brought another extinguisher from his trunk and handed it to another trucker to monitor the situation

"A rescue truck and two ambulances are on the way," he said. "There doesn't seem to be any serious bleeding or lack of breathing, so we will wait for them."

Brady hung around until the other emergency services arrived and then picked up the blanket that wasn't being used and went back to the Suburban. He stowed the blanket and got into the driver's seat.

"How are they?" Star asked.

"Don't know for sure. No blood to speak of and everyone was breathing. The Trooper thought it best to wait for the professionals before trying to get the others out. We aren't needed anymore so it's best if we get out of the way. Thanks for calling it in. We got a quick response."

"Yeah. The OnStar operator was great."

Brady eased the Suburban back onto the travel lanes and headed west once more. The sky was darkening despite the time of day, and the snow was getting heavier and heavier. Suddenly Star's cellular phone rang, making both of them jump.

"Hello?"

"Hi Daddy."

"What? But you can't! Don't you see what is going on? It's too dangerous!"

Brady couldn't make out what was said, but he could tell Star was getting a lecture from her father. Brady kept his concentration on the road. She seemed to be taking it well.

"Okay, Daddy. It's your life. But don't say I didn't warn you."

Star closed the cellular phone and sat quietly for some time.

"We don't really have to hurry. Daddy won't be there when we arrive. His new girlfriend just talked him into going on a world cruise. They've already left the port. Can you believe it? At a time like this!"

Brady made sympathetic noises. Star sat silently for several more minutes. "He's even closing up the house. I won't be able to stay there while he is gone. The staff will be gone by Monday. Rats. Hoisted on my own petard. I don't think he'd be going if I hadn't acted up again. My own fault. He did this once before, but only for a month. This is a good year, if he doesn't come back early. Which he probably will, but no telling when."

"What are you going to do for money? Did he cut you off? Or do you work?"

"I volunteer. I don't have to work. But Daddy didn't cut me off, anyway. Besides which, I do have money of my own. I just don't like to touch it. A trust fund from my Grandfather. It's just easier and more fun to live off Daddy. He insists on it, actually. Like I said, he loves me and I love him. We just show it in strange ways."

"Oh. So you'll be okay, then."

"Of course. I can take care of myself, when I want to."

Brady left it at that. Both fell quiet, lost in their own thoughts as they continued to listen to the news on the radio. The snow storm got worse and the stormy political situation did, too, even as they listened.

They ran out of the snow just before they got to Kansas City. Star gave Brady precise directions to her father's house. It was a big one, on five acres, in the very good section of town. Lots of glass. Star had Brady accompany her inside. He carried her bags, but gave them to a maid when she opened the door and reached for them.

"Come on back to the study. I'll get you that money. How much do you charge Parkinson for a delivery?"

"Seven-fifty a day, plus expenses. But you don't have to worry about that. He'll pay me."

"Oh, but I owe you. Triple I believe I said." Star had a safe behind a painting open and was taking out stacks of bills. That would be fifteen hundred a day for two days, plus expenses. Four thousand should cover it, shouldn't it? Including a tip."

"I'm not going to take your money. Parkinson will pay me. That's all I want."

Star smiled, but her eyes glinted. "I pay my debts. Late sometimes, but I pay them. I said I'd pay you triple and I will. Even if I have to buy something that can't be returned and give it to you. My next trip to St. Louis."

Brady didn't want to argue. He didn't want the money, but it was easier to take it than not. Besides, she could obviously afford it. Or her father could, at least. He could at least get a dig in. "Actually, I'd prefer it in gold, but cash will have to do."

"No," Star said. "That's not a problem. I'll check Kitco for the spot price."

"Are you telling my you… I mean your father keeps gold in the house?"

"Sure. He thinks I'll get kidnapped by foreign nationals and he'll have to buy me back using gold or diamonds. He's a little paranoid."

Star was opening up the laptop computer sitting on the desk. It was the work of only a couple minutes to go into kitco.com and get the spot price of gold. She converted it in her head, much to Brady's surprise, and then rose and went back to the still open safe.

"Six and three quarter ounces. You did a good job. We'll make it an even seven." Star took out a plastic coin tube that glowed golden. She counted out seven one ounce American Gold Eagles, and handed them to a speechless Brady. "I really do appreciate you doing what you did."

Brady managed a "No problem," but that was all. As Star began to close up the safe, Brady said, "I'll be going, then. Take care of yourself."

"Okay. Thank you, Brady. Brady, before you go, could you give me some tips about what to do if this war talk comes true?"

"Gee, Star! I don't think a few tips will help, but… buy non-perishable food, a lot of it. And get lots of water. And look for a place where you can shelter from fallout. Better yet, get out of town. Kansas City may or may not be a target. There are so many things that should be done. It's hard to prepare on short notice, even with plenty of money."

"I understand, Brady. Thanks for the advice. I'll walk you to the door."

Brady found himself reluctant to leave. Sure she was a grown woman and able to take care of herself. But still…

Then he was outside, walking to the Suburban. His conscience pricked him a bit as he drove away. He'd gone less than a block when he turned around and went back to the house. The maid let him in when he rang the bell. Star came walking in to see who it was. "Brady!" she exclaimed, obviously quite surprised to see him again.

"Look. I have a retreat in the Ozarks. If you want to go with me until this all blows over… since your father isn't here…"

"Really?" Star asked softly. "Even after all the trouble I've been?"

Brady nodded. It was enough for Star. She became all business. "What do I need to bring? Besides money." She was headed for the study. Brady followed along.

"I've got everything we need," he told her.

"I pay my way," she replied, going to the safe and opening it. She went to the credenza behind the desk, leaned down and took out a leather attaché case. She transferred everything in the safe to the case. "What else?"

"Camping gear if you have it."

"We use the motorhome. You think I should drive it down?"

"No. Be nice to have, but it would slow us down. I really want to get going."

"What about guns? All right if I bring one? Or two?"

Again Brady was surprised by Star. "One little one and one big one?" She pulled a Walther PPK from somewhere behind her back and showed it to him. "Daddy got it for me."

A little alarmed now, Brady quickly asked. "Can you shoot it effectively?"

"Oh, sure. I go to the range three or four times a year."

"Okay. You had that on the trip?"

Star nodded and re-holstered the PPK. Brady had to look hard to see its imprint on her shirt in the small of her back. He couldn't believe he hadn't picked up on the fact that she had apparently been carrying the entire time. There was even a spare magazine from the looks of it.

"And the big gun?" Brady asked.

"It's Daddy's actually, but it's the only long gun Daddy has here. It was a gift and he likes to keep it handy and look at it." Star went to a large wooden armoire and opened one of the tall doors. She took out a very expensive looking case and set it down on the desk. "Take a look. Should I even bring it?"

Brady opened the case. "Nice gift!" he said as he peered down at the beautifully engraved long arm. "A drilling," Brady said then, picking up the butt-stock and action from its compartment in the case.

"Actually," Star corrected him, "It's a vierling. There are four barrels, not three."

Brady picked up the barrels and looked in the chamber end. She was right. He checked the ammunition in the case. Apparently it was a double barrel twenty-gauge with a .308 Winchester barrel below, and a .22 Hornet just above the .308.

"It's a Heym Model 37V vierling," Star said. "Daddy looked it up after he got it. Over twenty-grand to have one made. He loves to admire it. Only shot it a couple of times. He let me shoot it once at the range. Several people shot it that day. The consensus was that it was 'Sweet'. I could see why they said it."

"Not a good defensive weapon, but a great hunting gun. Bring it if you want. Do you have any more ammunition for it?"

"In the armoire."

Brady went over to look and found two full boxes of twenty-gauge 7 ½ shot, two twenty-round boxes each of .308 and .22 Hornet hunting ammunition. There was also a partial box of each. Brady set it out. He noticed a wooden case, and on a hunch, checked it. It was a fancy gun cleaning kit. He set it on the desk, too.

Star put the two components back into their individual compartments in the case. A tooled leather sling was in another compartment, with a quick detach scope in another. Eight shotgun rounds and four each .308 and .22 Hornet occupied drilled holes in an upholstered ammunition block.

"This really should be kept in a gun safe," Brady said.

"Daddy thought about it, he said. But figured if he had one he'd just bring his collection home. He's trying to shy away from them. Politics and all, you know."

Brady decided not to get into that debate. "Put the ammo in your case and go get everything you want to take. I'll take these out to the truck. Will we need to go to your apartment, too?"

"No. I spend so much time here that everything important is kept here. The apartment is more for the show of independence. And to be by myself when I really want to be."

Brady waited in the entry hall for Star after he put the gun and ammunition in the Suburban. Star came around a corner carrying two large suitcases. The maid was behind her with two more.

Taking the two cases from the maid, despite her protest, he led the way out to the Suburban, Star following along with her two cases. "What do you have in here, bricks?" Brady asked as he hefted the first case into the back of the Suburban.

"Just girly things," Star replied.

Brady didn't reply. He just put the other bags in beside the first one.

"Just one more," Star said, headed back to the house, while Brady waited with the back door of the truck open.

She loaded it herself when she returned. Brady noted that Star was wearing a much heavier coat now, but was still in the blue jeans and blue shirt, and baseball cap. She'd changed shoes, too, from the jogging shoes she'd got at the mall for a comfortable looking pair of walking shoes.

"I'm ready," she said, shifting the large leather shoulder bag to a more comfortable position, and Brady closed the door.

With both of them in the Suburban, Brady set off. "You need to stop anywhere?"

"Yeah. My bank." Brady hated to use the time. China was invading and the US carriers were launching aircraft to intervene. They might not have much time. But he drove Star to her bank and waited in the Suburban while she went in. It seemed like forever to Brady, but it was just a few minutes.

Then he got a little annoyed, for when she came out she pointed to a shop next door to the bank, turned and went in. Brady couldn't make out what kind of shop it was, but if she came out carrying a fancy dress he was going to turn her over his knee. He was still contemplating how bad an idea that actually was when she hurried out of the store. She ran over to the Suburban and got in. She wasn't carrying anything, but since she said, "That's it. We'd better go. They had a radio on in the store. I'm getting really scared, Brady."

"Don't worry. We'll be safe at my retreat when we get there."

"Good. But we still have to get there before the world blows up. Thank you so much for bringing me along. You certainly didn't have to. I hope Daddy is okay."

Brady didn't reply. The snow storm had caught up with them. The blizzard would be on them before they reached Springfield, Brady was sure. And after that, if the forecast held true, they'd be out of the blizzard, sure, but had an ice storm to get through before they got to the retreat. He did take the time to top off the fuel tanks with diesel before they left Kansas City behind them.

They continued to listen to the radio as the miles and the hours passed. Brady was an experienced driver and had little trouble with the snow in the heavy, four-wheel-drive Suburban.

Suddenly Star said, "I noticed all the stuff on the Suburban. Can you tell me about it? It all looks so interesting."

Brady hesitated, but shrugged mentally. Star was going to the retreat. Wouldn't be many secrets left when they got there. "Sure. Stop me if I bore you."

"Don't worry," Star said with a laugh.

"Well, of course it started out as a standard four-wheel-drive three-quarter ton Chevy Suburban. It was stolen from the original owners by one of the Mexican drug gangs. They had some custom things done to it, like the snorkel and a winch under the front bumper. Larger fuel tanks replaced the original tank. Put a two inch lift under it. They had a light bar on top for driving lights. And some hidden compartments here and there. It was used as a carrier for cross border drug runs in remote areas.

"They finally got caught by the Border Patrol and the Suburban was impounded and put up for auction. I knew about it, of course, and put in a bid for it. Wasn't the Suburban's fault it had been used for illegal activities.

"I used it the way it was until I started prepping. I made a few changes after I learned about such things on the internet. Swapped the gasoline engine for a non-electronic diesel and had the frame reinforced. Instead of an alternator, I got an old fashioned 12 volt generator installed, along with an air pump, and hydraulic pump. I replace the original single battery with a two battery system for the 24-volt starter, using the biggest batteries that would fit. Plus, there is a third deep discharge 12-volt battery to run 12-volt equipment and an inverter.

Compressed air is piped to the front and rear bumpers so I can use air tools for changing tires and such. Ditto for the hydraulic system. Besides using it for tools, it supplies the power for the new hydraulic winch that replaced the 12 volt winch in the front bumper. I've got a portable hydraulic winch that slides into the rear receiver hitch."

Brady looked over at Star. She still looked interested, so Brady continued. "The same shop that replaced the engine installed heavier skid plates, and added a couple more. A welder friend made the heavy-duty custom bumpers. The front bumper, beside the winch, has the light guards I'm sure you saw, along with the additional lights and spare tire carrier. There is also a 2-inch receiver hitch under the bumper.

"The rear bumper has a 2-inch receiver hitch and swing away mounts for another spare tire, Hi-Lift jack, D-handle shovel, axe, pick-mattock, sledge hammer, and three five-gallon jerry cans of water.

"The heavy-duty top rack has more lights mounted around the edges and two remote control spot/flood lamps. The antennas for the communications gear are mounted on it, too. I don't carry much in it most of the time, because of fuel mileage, but there are a pair of aluminum bridging ramps, an extension ladder, and a third spare tire in it right now."

"These are custom bucket seats and console. As you can see, the communications and navigation gear are mounted in it, along with the auxiliary switches for the extra lighting.

"I have a couple toolboxes in back with tools, service items, and spare parts."

"Wow! You know, I almost bought a Hummer, once. Just for kicks. I think I like this better."

"Maybe you have the prepper gene," Brady said and Star laughed. Brady liked her laugh.

He kept up a steady pace, going south on Highway 13, occasionally passing a vehicle going slower than he was. Much of the traffic was going around him, but he'd already seen enough vehicles off in the ditch, many of them four wheel drive, than to drive the same way. And they hadn't even hit the ice yet.

Brady stopped and helped the first two vehicles they saw off the road, but there were just too many of them if they stopped and helped everyone. Emergency services vehicles, as well as maintenance vehicles were out in force. Brady decided to let them handle the job they were being paid to do. He quit stopping to help, even as the blizzard caught up and passed them.

He slowed down to a crawl in four-wheel-drive but was able to keep going. The state had been plowing the road so the snow wasn't too deep in the travel lanes yet, but it was building rapidly. They began to see more cars stopped. Not all of them were in the ditch. Some had just stopped in the travel lanes, afraid to go further in the blizzard.

Brady carefully drove around them until finally they saw no one else. They were the only thing still moving. The snow was almost up to the bumper on the front of the Suburban, but it was a light, dry snow and the truck was able to push through it with little trouble on the somewhat aggressive all-weather Toyo tires the Suburban sported.

Brady was about ready to pull to the shoulder and stop. The Suburban was losing traction occasionally now. But he decided to push on just a little bit further. He was glad he did, for in another mile they ran out of the snow fall like driving through a wall. There was only the lightest dusting of snow ahead of them.

Unfortunately, as they hit Springfield, they hit freezing rain and were right back down to a crawling pace. But Brady kept it up. They were on the home stretch. Though he still had plenty of fuel, he topped the tanks again, so they could take a break and get something to eat and warm to drink, before they continued.

"I don't see how you do it," Star said, as they left Springfield and picked up Highway 65 going south toward Branson. "I'd be a nervous wreck. I never would have made it through the snow, much less this. Especially in the motorhome."

"We aren't there yet."

"I'll shut up," Star said. "I am a jinx."

No sooner than she had said it than a car on an intersecting road couldn't stop and slid through the intersection. Brady had to swerve to miss it and the Suburban spun out, going down into the ditch on the right side. It still had a little bit of momentum and Brady floored the accelerator. The diesel engine roared and the Suburban began sliding all over, but Brady was able to get it back up onto the road.

"Holy cow!" Star said. "That was some driving!"

Brady looked back. The car had slid all the way across 65 and then kept going on the intersecting road. Brady wasn't sure the driver had even seen the Suburban. He got out into the freezing drizzle and walked around the Suburban, checking for damage, but couldn't see any.

After a bit to catch his breath he got back in the Suburban and continued the journey. Suddenly, just north of Branson, the radio went dead, and the vehicle that was ahead of them slowed, and pulled over to the shoulder of the road. Though the next vehicle was some distance ahead of them, Brady was sure it had stopped, too.

"This is it," Brady said grimly.

"What?" Star asked.

"I think we just got hit with an EMP surge. See the cars up ahead? They suddenly came to a stop. At the same time the radio went dead."

"Oh. How come we didn't stop?"

"No critical electronic parts on the engine. EMP proof. But not the radio." They were coming up on the first stranded vehicle. A woman was out in the cold, coat clutched around her, staring the engine under the open hood of the car.

"Brady…" Star started to say.

He was already pulling over to stop. Star got out of the Suburban this time with Brady. "Come on, Lady," Brady called. "We'll take you in to Branson. You aren't going to get it to start."

She didn't ask why, just hurried to the back door of the car and backed out a few seconds later carrying a baby in a child carrier seat. Brady took the child from her when she slipped and almost fell. Star helped her to the passenger side of the Suburban while Brady went to the driver's side rear passenger door and set the baby carrier on the seat. The mother leaned over and began to fasten the carrier into place with the seatbelt. Brady and Star climbed back into the Suburban and Brady got it moving again.

He also stopped at the second vehicle. It was a man alone. Brady offered to give him a ride in, but the man refused, saying his brother-in-law was traveling behind him and would help him get the car going. His brother-in-law was a crackerjack mechanic, according to the man.

Brady looked over at Star. She shrugged.

"I feel bad," Brady said when he got back into the truck. "But he really insisted on staying to wait for his brother."

"Can't save people from themselves," Star said.

The mother asked from the back seat, "What's going on? I just thought my car quit, though it just had a tune up, but with this other one at the same time…"

"I think we've been attacked with an EMP weapon," Brady said.

"What's that?" the mother asked. "What do you mean, attacked?"

"It's a nuclear device enhanced to knock out electronics in a wide area," Brady said. "Did you notice your radio went dead at the same time the car died?"

"Yes… I guess it did, but I didn't really notice. Nuclear device? Do you mean atomic bombs? We were attacked with atomic bombs? That can't be! That just can't be!"

Brady had to concentrate on his driving. Star twisted around in her seat and began trying to calm the mother as the baby slept peacefully, oblivious of what was going on. Whatever Star had said to the mother seemed to work. She was sitting quietly, cooing to the baby when they came up on another stopped vehicle.

This time it was a man, woman, and child. Brady offered to take them the rest of the way to Branson and they accepted, the man saying, "Cell phone won't work out here. They guaranteed it. I'll be talking to them, believe you me!"

Neither Brady nor Star tried to explain this time. Brady just made room in the back of the Suburban for the father and son. The mother rode beside the other woman. They didn't see anyone else and were soon in Branson. It was cold and raining, but no more ice. Both families lived in Branson and Brady dropped them off, warning them that they should try to find a radio that would work and find out what was going on. He refused to explain further.

Star took note of Brady's still grim expression and repeated her earlier assertion. "You can't save people from themselves."

"I know. But that baby…"

"Try not to think about it," Star said softly. She didn't admit that the baby's fate was in her thoughts, too.

Another forty minutes and they were at the compound.

"You have a castle!"

"Not exactly," Brady said.

"Sure looks like a castle. Kind of short though."

"It's not a castle." Brady had already been kidded about being King of the Castle after the crenellated parapet wall had been installed. Brady drove up, past the gravel parking lot half full of vehicles, mostly cars, though with a mix of pickups and SUV's, as well as two Class C motor homes.

Brady was pleased to note that the compound had been secured. The main gate was closed and he assumed it was locked. The gate was in two parts that rolled open and closed on V-grooved steel wheels that ran on inverted angle-iron set in concrete. The wheeled, steel caged concrete bases supported walls of the same type of bullet and fire resistant construction that most of the community buildings did, only thicker.

Star noted an unusual feature of the gates. One of the walls had a large circular opening in it just above the base. It was filled in, but Star couldn't for the life of her figure out why it was there.

CHAPTER SIX

Getting out of the Suburban Brady walked over to the gate and gave a password. The gates began to open. Brady drove through them when they were wide enough apart and they began to close again. There was a concrete parking lot off to one side of the gate opening and Brady pulled into it. Star looked back at the gate. Where the circle was on the outside of the gate was a pipe sticking out at least three feet from the wall. Some type or rod or pipe was centered in it.

Star suddenly noticed people walking along the top of the walls, behind the parapets. They were all carrying rifles on slings over their shoulders. Every so often one or another of them would stop and look out at the forest encircling the place with a pair of binoculars.

Brady saw Barbara running over toward the Suburban. She came to an abrupt halt when Star opened her door and stepped out. She regained her composure quickly and hurried up to Brady to give him a big hug. Brady had to lean over for her, since she was seven months pregnant.

"Who all has made it in?" Brady asked.

"Only about half," Barbara replied. "We haven't heard from anyone since the EMP."

"Barbara, this is Star. Star Barbara. She's number two in command here." Brady introduced them to one another as he came around the front of the Suburban. "Any hard news?"

"Nothing was announced before we lost communications. No activity on the radiation meters. But the airways are just screaming with static. Occasionally we'll hear a burst of it. Dwayne doesn't know if that is just natural for an ionized atmosphere or an indication that more warheads are hitting."

Star blanched. They were talking about it so matter-of-factly. She was terrified, but she stood there and listened.

"Okay," Brady said. "Get everyone not already in the blast shelter inside. I'll take the watch for a while. No need to risk any more people outside than necessary. Take the Suburban over to the women's dorm and get Star settled there, then into the shelter with the others.

"I'd rather stay with you," Star said.

Barbara looked on, fascinated.

"Of course not," Brady said.

"I can help. I owe you for bringing me. Better me at risk than people that have planned this. They deserve the best chance possible to get through it."

Brady could tell she was scared, but she offered anyway. And she was always adamant about carrying her own weight. "All right. But don't make me regret it." He turned to Barbara. Have one of the sentries give Star their binoculars and radio as you send them down. Star, you're on sentry duty. Just walk the parapets and scan the forest methodically in each direction. You see anyone coming, sing out."

Again he turned to Barbara. "The GMRS radios did come through all right, didn't they?"

"Yes," Barbara replied. "But with the static they barely reach across the compound."

"That's all we need at the moment," Brady replied. "Get me one, too."

Barbara hurried off. Star followed behind. Each of the sentries that came down protested, but Brady sent them to the blast shelter. The compound was where it was in part because there were no perceived targets close. But Brady had never trusted to the fact that all the missiles would hit their intended targets. It seemed likely to him that at least some would malfunction and that meant they were as likely to hit nearby as far away.

Brady watched Star for a few moments. She was doing as he asked. He had barely walked back to the Suburban to take it to his housing unit to unload his stuff when the radio in his pocket squealed.

"Someone coming up the road," Star said. He looked over at her and she pointed toward the road.

Brady hurried over to the gate. He opened the spy panel in one of the gates. It was Dr. Amos. He opened the Cadillac's door and put one foot on the ground raising his head above the roof. He gave the password and Brady operated the gate controls. They could be opened by hand, but it was a struggle. They'd tried to EMP proof as much of the key electrical circuits as they could. Apparently at least some of the methods had worked.

Brady spoke into the radio, calling for Barbara. "Dr. Amos is here. Send someone out to help. Not you. You're restricted to the blast shelter for the duration, and no arguments."

Barbara didn't protest. She had the unborn baby to worry about. She sent one of the men.

When Brady checked, Star was making her rounds. She hadn't stayed to watch.

Brady let three more sets of people in when Star called him on the radio and said she had to go to the bathroom. "Okay," Brady said. "I think it's time to get into the shelter. Anyone else that comes up will have to use the alternate signal to get one of us out of the shelter to let them in. We're just taking too big of a risk. It's been two hours since the EMP. Maybe the war is over now. Maybe not. Just come on down."

When she reached the bottom of the nearest stairway up to the ramparts, Brady joined her to show her the way into the shelter. As Brady took the first step the sky lit up behind them. He grabbed Star's hand and began to run without saying a word. Terror lent wings to Star's feet. She stayed up with him as he headed for the exterior entrance to the blast shelter. The heavy door was already closing. It should have already been closed, but Brady never said anything about it. He and Star would probably have been dead if they had not delayed closing the door.

The residents of the blast shelter felt it move as the ground wave hit. Sounds of blast valves closing on the air intakes told of the presence of the blast wave arriving seconds later. Brady was glad they worked. They should already have been closed manually.

Everyone looked around at everyone else. All knew that the nuclear blast had to have been relatively close. Several people called out to Brady and Star. "What direction? What direction?"

"Southeast," Brady said. Many people let out sighs of relief. The wind was blowing from the north at the moment, but was usually from the west. They should miss much of the fallout, though certainly not all of it, as close as they were to the blast.

"Hey! Hey!" yelled the man manning the communications console. "There's someone at the gate!"

"I need two people," Brady called. Half a dozen men stood up or moved forward.

"I'll go," Star said, stepping toward the blast door.

Brady didn't feel he had time to argue. The remote reading radiation survey meter was still silent and still. No radiation yet. But that nearby blast would be dumping some on them soon. Brady pointed to one of the men and turned away. He, the man, and Star ran out when one of the others opened the blast door. "Close it," he ordered. "Open it only on the password."

The three hurried to the main gate and Brady checked the peep hole. "Geez! It's Holly Hamston! And she's hurt.

George, the other man, worked the gate controls and Brad and Star ran out. Holly was lying on the ground, covered in blood. Her car was upside down, resting against the wall near the gate. Brady took a quick look at the nearest forest. There were lots of trees down from the blast wave and ground shock.

George ran over to check the car. There was another person in it. A child. But George could tell he was dead. He ran back to help Brady with Holly. They would have to get a stretcher or risk further injuring her.

"Brady," Star said, reaching behind her to touch him on the shoulder. "Several people are coming. On foot."

He took a quick look. They were still too far away for Brady to recognize any of them. But they made their identity known. Those in the forefront of the group raised rifles and began to run forward, firing as they came.

"Crimeny," Brady said. He drew his Glock and pumped several rounds toward the group, not expecting to hit anyone, but hoping to slow them down. "Come on, George! We have to get her inside." Both men reached down and grabbed her under the arms. Brady steadied her head as they drug her toward and through the gate.

Star was firing her PPK at the still approaching crowd as she backed toward the gate. George and Brady gently put Holly down and both jumped toward the gate controls. They were almost closed when Star yelped and fell down. Brady pulled out his radio and keyed the mike. "I need a medical team and a security team on the double."

Star sat on the ground, groaning, her hands wrapped around her left thigh. Blood was oozing from a hole in her jeans. Brady ran for the steps to get up behind the parapets to see where the advancing group was.

As soon as he showed his face between the merlons he had to duck back. Someone had taken a shot at him. He picked another spot and eased he head around for a quick look. The group was milling around, a hundred feet away, apparently trying to decide what to do.

"Hey!" Brady yelled and ducked behind a merlon when he saw one of the group raise a rifle. A shot rang out. Brady had no idea where it went, but he stayed behind the merlon as he called out again. "What do you want?" He realized how ridiculous the question was even as he asked it.

"Let us in! We know you have shelter! We want in!"

Brady took another quick look. They were still milling around, several of those with weapons had them trained on the parapet. He changed positions again and then directed the dozen armed men and women that had joined him to spread out. He sent three to keep an eye on the rest of the area surrounding the compound.

"We don't have room for all of you," Brady called down to the group. "Send in your women and children and then go look for shelter elsewhere. I suggest you hurry."

"It's all or nothing!" screamed one of the men. He fired at the parapets again, and there came a fusillade of rounds as his companions did the same thing.

"Open fire," Brady called to his group, resulting in a flurry of shots from both sides, with half a dozen of the group outside falling down. The rest scrambled for the concealment of the trees. Brady's group continued to fire until there were no more targets in sight. Three more men went down.

"Everyone okay?" Brady asked, moving down the line. They had sustained nothing more than some concrete dust in the face of one of the women from a ricochet. Dust began to fall from the darkening sky.

Brady's radio buzzed and he keyed it. "Brady."

"We're getting radiation readings now. Low, but climbing steadily. You've got to get everyone inside."

"Okay." Brady signaled the others and directed them to head for the shelter. They scrambled to obey, the dust coming down more heavily every second.

"Brady! Hurry!" came Barbara's voice from the radio. "The radiation just jumped to 2,000R!"

"Last chance!" Brady yelled over to the tree line. "Send the women and children!" His answer was another fusillade of shots. Brady headed for shelter.

He had to wait for his turn in the decontamination room off the main entrance to the blast shelter. When he was decontaminated and in clean clothes, Brady hurried over to the communications station. He checked the AMP-200 high range survey meter. Already up from 2,000 to 2,500 and the digital readout was scrolling the numbers higher as they watched.

"Geez!" Brady said softly. There was nothing he could do for those outside. Even if he did let them in most would die from the massive doses they were receiving now. He would undoubtedly become sick himself, though he didn't think he'd received a deadly dose. He felt like kicking himself for not having clipped on a dosimeter before he went outside.

Brady suddenly remembered Holly and Star. He went over to the area set aside as the infirmary. One of the nurses that were part of the MAG stopped Brady. "Dr. Amos is attending to Star."

"What about Holly?" Brady asked.

The woman shook her head. "The injuries were just too bad. I don't think we could have saved her with a full trauma ward."

Brady waited, rather impatiently, until Dr. Amos came out from behind the curtain that delineated the infirmary.

"How is she, Doc?" he immediately asked.

"She's resting. I gave her a pain killer and antibiotics. It was a through and through so I didn't have to go in for the bullet. She should be okay in a few days."

Brady breathed a sigh of relief.

Dr. Amos continued. "I'm sorry about the other woman… Holly, wasn't it? We tried, but…"

"The nurse told me. Did you take care of it?

Dr. Amos nodded. "Body bag is in the designated area for burial when we get out."

"Can I see Star?" Brady asked.

"She'll be a bit woozy, but okay. Don't take too long."

Brady nodded and stepped behind the curtain. Star was on a cot, a blanket up to her chin. Her eyes were a little dull as she turned them to Brady. They seemed to brighten slightly at the sight of him. "You okay?" she asked her voice a little slurred.

"I'm fine. The doctor said you were going to be fine, too."

"I know. He told me. I'm kind of tired. Could you sit with me for a few minutes?"

Brady hurried to get a chair and bring back to her bedside. She reached out her hand and Brady took it gently in his. It was only a minute or so and she was asleep. He sat there and watched her for several more minutes and then Brady eased her hand back onto the edge of the cot. He got up and went to check on things in the blast shelter.

He found Harry. "What's the inside reading?"

"Under 0.05.

"Air?"

"Filters are working good. On battery right now."

"Any signs of damage from the blast wave and ground shocks?"

"Not in here," Harry replied. "How about Topside?"

"Didn't notice anything in the compound. Quite a few trees down. Didn't really notice if the antenna towers were still up or not. How about comms? The faraday cage work?"

"Don't know yet. Wanted to wait a bit, just in case of another EMP. We're thinking about hooking up a broadband to an external antenna once in a while to check for a few minutes and then unhook and ground the antenna lead again. Minimal risk."

"Good idea. Do it."

"When do you think we can disperse to the other shelters? Even without full occupancy we're crowded."

"I want to give it a day. Wait for the radiation to begin falling and wait out a second attack. Everyone get potassium iodate?"

"Yeah. Doc Started handing them out as soon as he got here.

Barbara came up to them then. "Boss, we've got a census and set up sleeping and eating schedules." She went over the list of names of those that had made it to the compound. And those that had not. Brady could only hope they'd found expedient shelter and would be able to make it to the compound after the radiation faded.

"What do you think is going on out there?" Barbara asked, nodding toward the entryway.

"I'm sure some of that group are trying to get in. Probably will with no one defending the place. I just hope they don't do too much damage. Everything is locked up. I doubt they have any tools except for their weapons. What I can't figure is how they survived the blast wave."

Barbara thought for a moment. "If they were in that low spot just before the turn into our road, they might have been fairly well protected. Think they'll try to break in here?"

"Possibly. But they won't be able to without explosives. And then we can destroy them in the entry airlock as they come in," Brady said grimly. He would have helped as many of the group as he could, the women and children, if they'd just tried to cooperate. But they had decided to try to take over the place. That wasn't going to happen.

The group settled in for the duration. Brady had planned well. They had everything they needed in the shelter. After the radiation had peaked at nearly 10,000R/hr and then dropped rapidly to under 1,000R/hr, Brady decided to let the primary investors move to their own basement shelters if they wanted. He felt the risk of another nearby burst was very unlikely. As it was, even the basement shelters provided significant blast protection.

So the hatches to the tunnel system were opened and people used the automotive crawlers Brady had purchased to move to the other shelters to ride out the rest of the wait time until they could go outside.

All those that had been outside when the fallout started showed the early symptoms of radiation poisoning. Nausea and/or vomiting the first day or so, with Brady suffering the most. Some became lethargic and lost some hair in the two weeks following, again with Brady having the worst of it. Everyone else was fine.

They settled in for the long haul. Based on the seven ten rule, which the actual radiation readings were confirming, it would be five months before considerable time could be spent outside, with it being a full year before they could expect to leave the shelter permanently. However, after a month Brady sent out a team to check on the compound.

The team suited up in Tyvek environmental suits, rubber boots and gloves, and Millennium CBRN respirators. They were on a fifteen minute time limit as the radiation was just below 5R/hr.

All the faces were ashen when the team came in, and gave their report after they decontaminated. Brady, Harry, Barbara, and Dr. Amos listened as the team described what they'd seen.

The gates were still closed, the power having been cut off during the attack. Some men had been able to scale the walls and gain entrance to the compound, but they had not been able to open the gates manually. There was a hidden braking system on both gate panels.

There were bodies everywhere, singly and in groups, both inside and outside the compound. Dead from the radiation it looked like in most of the cases, plus a few shootings that had taken place after the compound residents had taken shelter. There were signs of the people having tried to enter the primary housing units, without success.

"There were women and kids all in a group, just outside the gates," one of the team said, and then broke down, crying. It was a near thing for the rest. Dr. Amos took charge, leading the team over to another of the doctors in the group that had a lot of psychological training.

"Should we send out another team to do something with the bodies?" Harry asked.

Brady shook his head. "Not now. It won't make any difference to the dead, and we have to save radiation doses for more important things, just in case." The command group broke up, going their own ways. Brady was staying in the blast shelter while the others in the command structure, all primary investors, had gone to their own shelters.

Brady spent a lot of his time talking to the recuperating Star. She was able to get around on crutches. The wound was healing nicely, but it itched and she had a tendency to scratch at it without thinking about it. Brady himself was recuperating from the radiation poisoning. He was very weak and lethargic. Talking to Star raised his spirits. She was full of stories about her life growing up wealthy in Kansas City.

The first five months passed and groups began going out, fully suited, and for limited times. Only those in the lowest potential risk category went out. Those that were older, mostly, for the residual effects would probably not show up in them until late in their lives. The young, and those that had already received doses, were exempted until the radiation fell to lower levels. Brady chafed at not being able to go out, but he was high risk now, with the exposure he'd had and the resulting depression of his immune system.

Fortunately they were well stocked with medical grade masks. The doctors ordered everyone to wear one when they were in the blast shelter among the large group, to reduce the risk of spreading any infections. Even given that, mild cold symptoms spread through most of the population of the blast shelter. Those that were staying in their own shelters were for the most part spared that.

The teams began the cleanup and decontamination. The decontamination was made much easier with the designs of the building and compound, and the equipment they had on site. Because of the limited times each group could be out it took some time to do the decontamination, even as easy as it was with what they had.

Using the light construction equipment Brady had provided the MAG a mass grave was dug and the bodies of the dead were buried out near the trees where most of them had died. Holly and her son got individual graves in an area Brady had set aside for such cases. No one had known about it until Brady brought it up.

The farmers stripped a thin layer of soil off the garden area and began putting in the garden when spring arrived. They didn't have much hope for it. The sky was cloudy more often than not, and the temperatures were not coming up the way they should, even for early spring. They did get quite a bit of spring rain. It carried a tiny amount of fine fallout particles, less and less with each rain.

Juan Mendoza moved back to his farm. People had been making trips to see about the animals. Some had survived in the shelters the MAG had had built. Juan had left plenty of feed and water for them. But there were still heavy losses. The compound's own animals came through without a problem in their earth sheltered barn.

The communications people had to replace a couple of antennas, though the heavy duty free-standing towers had come through with shining colors. The amateur radio operators in the group kept the command team informed on what was going on in the rest of the world. It wasn't much. It had been global nuclear war. Even the Southern Hemisphere had taken some hits with nuclear weapons, including Australia, Africa, and South America, though not nearly to the degree of the Northern Hemisphere.

The Swedes and Swiss had come out the best, with their extensive Civil Defense Preparedness Programs. Russia and the Republics had managed to shelter much of their population, but had lost almost all of their infrastructure, including many of their underground factories.

China had attacked Europe as well as North America and the Russian Republics. She had been hammered in return, by the US, Russia, Great Britain, and France. The Republics had also hit Europe hard after an initial delay, and Great Britain, France, and the US had responded.

The Middle East became one huge battlefield. Nuclear weapons from both sides flew, but when all were gone, ground forces began battling. It was ongoing. Just as it had been for the past many centuries. Essentially the same thing happened in Africa. Not that many nukes, but all the old tribal rivalries came to the fore without the interference of United Nations Peacemakers. Most of Africa actually did revert to near the Iron Age.

South Korea was overrun by the North, and China managed to take Taiwan, despite the efforts of the US Carrier Task Forces. They ran out of munitions and had to retreat. Both Task Forces were nuked, causing the loss of one of the carriers and most of the support ships. Only the submarines operated with impunity. Those on the high seas, anyway. All known US submarine support bases were hit with multiple warheads. Several subs were caught entering and leaving the area and were lost.

The American hunter/killer submarines had several field days. They were taking out opposing subs and surface ships right and left until they too ran out of munitions. The subs that the hunter/killers didn't get the ASW destroyers and frigates did.

The information came to the compound in bits and pieces over time. Initially they only knew what happened locally.

As the radiation levels continued to fall those in the compound began to make excursions further and further from the compound, using the small fleet of vehicles Brady had provided. Of all the vehicles brought by MAG members only one ran after the EMP attack. A young single man's diesel converted Jeep Wrangler.

Branson was almost deserted. Most of the surrounding farms were as well. The group managed to corral surviving stock animals and add them to Juan's herds and flocks.

Three more MAG members and their families showed up after the local radiation level had fallen to less than one. They'd agreed to run together. Car trouble for one of them delayed their arrival long enough that they had to take local shelter. Fortunately they were far enough away that the local blast didn't affect them. They received minor fallout from the west and northwest, but managed to shelter safely in a small town city hall basement.

When they began to travel after their local radiation dropped below 0.1R/hr, they would stop if they hit an area with higher radiation levels until it fell to a safer level, or they would try to go around.

All three families had been avid campers and were able to carry all the supplies and equipment they'd had in their vehicles on bicycles. Some which one family had brought with them, and some scavenged.

Every member of the small group suffered serious radiation poisoning symptoms, but only one of them died after they got to the compound. The others had to stay in the primary shelter unit they were sharing most of the time. They were just too weak to contribute to the work and would be for some time. Dr. Amos and the other medical people watched them carefully and treated them the best they could without a hospital.

Star, on the other hand, as soon as she could get about without the crutches and too much pain, threw herself into work. Brady had to sharply limit her outside access in the early days, much to her dismay. Even when inside she was usually helping the two teachers the MAG had as members with the children while their parents were working or taking some time for themselves.

The garden didn't do well that summer and fall. Most of the plants were disked into the soil. The three green houses, with grow light augmenting what natural sunlight there was did very well. Every inch of growing space inside was being used.

Juan had moderate success with his oil crop, but he managed to make over a thousand gallons of biodiesel over and above what the farm and the compound used that year. It was set aside for trading purposes.

They did some trading with some of the other local survivalist compounds as contacts were made with them through radio communications and exploration trips. There had been quite a few similar groups in the area. Not all of them had fared well, Brady learned.

One of the first Brady's MAG checked on was the one to which LaRhonda belonged. They had made it through the heavy fallout, but one of the members had been ill when she arrived and severe flu ran through the entire group. LaRhonda was one of only a dozen members out of thirty that survived it.

Brady set up an agreement with Sam Fellows, who had also survived the flu. Their animals had come through without a problem. Sam's MAG had a barn very similar to Brady's. They needed manpower and fuel. They had run their generator almost constantly when everyone was sick and dying. Brady's MAG would get additional firewood, animal food products, and propane. One of Sam's MAG members ran a propane business and had brought a semi-load and two delivery truck loads with him when he and his family bugged out to their compound.

Another compound went through the same thing as Sam's. They joined forces, the other camp moving lock, stock, and barrel to Sam's.

One of the main reasons for the excursions, besides making group contacts, was to find as many delivery trucks as they could and recover useable supplies. Branson was a tourist attraction and didn't have all that much useable goods, compared to its size. But they did need constant re-supply of consumables, so Brady and his group were able to scavenge quite a bit.

Brady's MAG was light on people like truck drivers so more agreements were set up with Sam's MAG and some of the others to share the resources found with the other MAG's providing the drivers and mechanics while Brady's group, with the most fuel and operable vehicles did the scouting and much of the labor. They also provided for the health care of several of the MAG's that didn't have medical personnel. The doctors and nurses made their own arrangements for trades and barters.

There had been no city, county, or state government left to speak of, and the feds were staying in the cities and just outside to try to get some semblance of infrastructure going again. Remote communities were left to their own devices. Which suited most of the MAG's in the Ozark Mountains. They were doing okay for themselves for the most part. The weather was still crappy, and Brady's MAG's greenhouse goods were in great demand.

CHAPTER SEVEN

Brady and Star were taking a casual stroll along the parapet wall, as was their wont from time to time. Not on duty, just enjoying being out. They felt a jolt and Brady grabbed Star to steady her as the ground and the wall shook for long moments.

"Wow!" Star said. "Earthquake!"

The two hurried down off the rampart and away from the wall in case an aftershock toppled it, as unlikely as that was. They looked around. People were coming out of all the buildings to see what was going on.

Everyone waited tensely, but no aftershock came. Finally Brady and Star headed to the blast shelter, where the communications gear was still kept. "Any reports?" he asked as soon as he came in.

"Yeah. Everyone local seems to have felt it. I'm running the HF amateur bands to see how wide spread it was."

Brady and Star sat and listened as the amateur began to contact their list of operating stations around the US. "Funny," Amanda said after talking to quite a few people. "I figured it was the New Madrid fault, and the early communications kind of supported that. But I'm not getting anything from Wyoming or the Dakotas. There were a lot of survivors up there."

"Yellowstone!" Brady said half under his breath.

"What?" asked Star.

"Yellowstone Caldera," Brady explained. "It's been acting up the last few years. It's one of the super volcanoes volcanologists have recently discovered. If it has blown big time, it is going to be bad."

"Even here?" Star asked, skeptically.

"Possibly. Probably. Not a lava flow, of course, but ash. Lots of ash. Possibly toxic ash."

"How soon?" Star suddenly believed Brady.

"Probably a day or more. We have time to get the hatches battened down." Brady turned back to Amanda. "Keep us informed." With that he headed out of the shelter. Star followed.

Brady began to gather people together, sending some to get others. Star stood beside him as he began to explain what he thought was going on.

"What about our people that are out helping the other MAG's?" was the first question that came up after he finished describing the probable effects of a super volcano explosion and how it might affect them here.

"I'm going now to get on the radio with the other compounds," Brady replied. "We'll recall all of our people as soon as we can. Start getting things ready, like you would for fallout dust."

"Star," Brady said as the group began to disperse, "I didn't see Barbara. She's probably napping with the baby. Would you go check on her and fill her in?"

"Sure, Brady." Star hurried toward Barbara's family's housing unit as Brady headed back to the blast shelter.

He sat down beside Amanda and got on one of the radios kept tuned to the frequency used for communications between the compounds.

Brady talked to each of the leaders, or their seconds-in-command, of all the MAG's with which they had contact. There was mostly disbelief, though all had felt the earthquake. All agreed to send Brady's people home as soon as possible.

With his people all accounted for Brady relaxed a little, but was soon up and supervising the preparations. Barbara left Jamie and Jane in the capable hands of the school teachers and went with Star to help with the preps. There wasn't that much to do, but volcanic dust is abrasive and often times corrosive. Everything was put under cover that could be. A couple of tools were made up to brush ash from the tops of the greenhouses if it started to build up. Brady didn't think it would, but the greenhouses were an extremely important part of their food production and he wasn't going to take any chances with them.

Routes were planned to allow the equipment to plow important areas clear of the ash. Part of Brady's initial planning had involved volcanoes. He had the materials on hand to make a pair of large cyclone air pre-filter systems for two of the U500 Unimogs. He put their machinist and welder on the job. The snow plows were attached and the trucks parked, ready to go.

Long handled brushes were made similar to the greenhouse ones to clean the windows on the Unimogs, since they would very likely be used during the ash fall. Using the regular wipers could easily scratch the glass as they dragged the abrasive volcanic dust across the windshield. It might not be much of a problem, since the windshields on the Unimogs were nearly vertical in orientation. But again, Brady wasn't taking chances.

All the air handling systems in the buildings were cleaned and filters cleaned or replaced. Large pre-filters were fitted to the air intakes using up much of their stock of spare HVAC filters.

And then they waited. All the rest of that day, and all the next day. People were beginning to wonder if Brady had been wrong and began grumbling about not being able to go about their regular business. All doubts vanished that Friday morning when the ash began to fall. It was worse than any blizzard any of them had ever been in. It was dark as night. The ash cloud blocked out all sunlight.

The ash fall started heavy and it continued heavy. At rates up to four inches an hour. Four people suited up as they had for the fallout decontamination and went to the Unimogs to start clearing the inside of the compound of the first layers of ash. They continued to go out from time to time to do so as the ash fall continued unabated for three full days and nights.

The accumulation rate fell drastically after the third night, and the sky brightened, but ash continued to fall lightly for another week. They had kept the open areas of the compound cleaned very well during the time the ash was falling. It would be months before they got rid of the accumulations in all the nooks and crannies.

Brady suited up one day and used the Bobcat A300 with bucket to cut a short trench out in the deepest part of the ash fall outside the compound so he could measure it. Approximately four feet, eight and one-half inches had fallen in total. The working areas of the property were cleared, as well as the area around the compound.

It was going to be years before some of the areas around the property not used heavily were cleared. It was all the two Unimogs could do to clear a single lane to Juan's farm. They tried using the big snow blowers they had for the Unimogs, but the blade wear was too great. As it was, using the snow plows was eating them up, but they were much more easily repaired.

The sunny days had been scarce before the volcano. Now they were nearly non-existent. The sky was hazy all the time. Even after it rained. And it rained a great deal. The rain did wash much of the ash away, at least on sloped ground. Large areas were cleared, the ash moving to the adjacent low spots, filling entire creek beds and gullies, even entire small valleys. In places the ash accumulated to thirty, forty, fifty feet and more.

And when it was still freshly wet it was like quick sand, though after it consolidated and the water began to run over the top of it rather than into it, it would hold up a person, but a vehicle would mire up immediately. Star found out the hard way when she and a team were on the way to check on one of the compounds with which they had lost contact.

The road she was driving on in Brady's Suburban was clear most of the way. Star had been able to drive across a couple of low places in the road that were covered with ash. When she came to a point where the road dipped down into a swale Star assumed she could cross it. The ash was much deeper here than what it looked and the road was clear on the other side of the ash flow, perhaps a quarter of a mile away.

Star did ease onto the flow, but when it seemed solid she continued. By another six feet the front of the Suburban went down to the winch and Star stopped. Everyone got out and struggled back to the exposed pavement. The Suburban was still sinking, much to Star's chagrin. She called it in to the compound and Brady sent one of the Unimogs out to pull the Suburban free.

"I'm sorry," she said as soon as Brady stepped down out of the passenger door of the Unimog.

"Stuff happens," he said softly. "Don't let it bother you. I knew this was going to happen eventually. Though not with my Suburban." Star blushed.

The Unimog easily pulled the Suburban out after they extended a cable to the trailer hitch of the Suburban. It had quit sinking when the tires had contacted the pavement under the ash. Brady had brought several five gallon buckets of water with Unimog and he started to get under the Suburban to clean the goo from the operating parts of the drive train.

Star saw what he was doing and insisted on doing it herself. She was covered with the stuff when she finally crawled out from under the truck. Brady took off the coveralls he had on over his regular clothing and gave them to Star to put on over her soiled things so she could ride in the cab of the Unimog rather than the back. She wanted to continue on the trip, but Brady insisted she go back to the compound and get cleaned up as soon as possible. The volcanic ash was proving mildly hazardous to the skin.

When Brady returned with the team later she was almost glad she'd got the Suburban stuck. Brady said it was bad at the other compound. None of the team said very much, but it was obvious from what they did say that the other compound was a total loss, with a total loss of life. Ash flow from the rains had scoured the side of the hill clean, taking buildings and all to the bottom of the valley. It must have happened suddenly. There were no signs at all of any survivors.

That was the worst occasion of the ash flow, but as contact was resumed Brady's group found out that several of the other MAG's, with compounds on the down side of the hilly country had suffered different degrees of the same thing.

Sam's compound was still cut off. There were low spots on both entrance roads that were filled to the brim with the ash. They were digging out, but it was going to take a while. Brady dispatched a Unimog with a backhoe mounted to help when he found out.

From what information they were able to gather from the surrounding countryside, a good twenty percent of the post war survivors in the area perished due to the ash fall and it's after effects. And that was before the winter set in.

The Ozarks occasionally suffered a severe winter, for, as Brady said one time, there wasn't anything between the North Pole and them but a few four strand barbed wire fences. A person from Alaska would have been right at home in Branson that winter.

The snow fell like the ash and the rains had. Often and heavily. Again the various compounds that were mutually supporting each other were physically cut off from one another. They were able to maintain radio contact much more effectively than they had during the ash fall.

One of the groups went completely silent in January after asking for shipments of food. All efforts to contact them failed. Not even Brady's group could conquer the snow and get to them.

As soon as the snow had diminished enough for the Unimog snowplows to make a dent in it, Brady headed out with as much food as they could spare, and two doctors and a nurse. It took two days to get to the compound. They found that they were too late. It looked like an internal battle had been fought over the last of the food. Not everyone died of hunger. More than a few had gunshot wounds.

Brady had all the bodies they could find moved into one room of one of the houses and the compound stripped of everything useable. They would come back in the spring to bury the bodies.

Spring finally rolled around, though late was hardly the word for it. Shortly after the snow began to melt quickly under spring rains two more compounds fell silent. There had been no pleas for help from either one of them. It was the two most remote of the MAG's, about equidistant from Sam's compound and Brady's.

They each sent a team to one of the compounds. Brady and his team reached their assigned compound first. It was deserted except for three dead bodies lying out in the open, hands and ankles tied, riddled with bullets. Two men and a woman. All three looked gaunt. One of the men Brady recognized as Colonel Machabee, leader of the group. It was comprised mostly of ex-military and their families.

They looked around the compound. It seemed to have been abandoned quickly, for there were still many useful items left, including a pair of generators and a full PV set up with battery bank and inverters. One of the generators was running. The compound still had running water. The kitchens were devoid of all food.

Brady shook his head. Other than the three dead people, there were no signs of a battle. There were no vehicles in evidence. Back in the Suburban, Brady picked up the microphone to call Sam and tell him what they'd found. Before he could key the mike the radio squealed and a woman's voice came out of the speaker. "We're taking fire! We're taking fire! People are down! People are down!" There were sounds of gunshots in the background and then the radio went silent.

"Saddle up!" Brady called to his team. He led the way at the highest speed they could maintain toward the other compound. He called the compound on the radio and had them go to a defensive posture. Brady heard Sam's voice on the radio doing the same with his compound. At least Brady knew Sam was still alive.

They came up on Sam's small convoy headed toward them at high speed. Both groups came to a halt and Brady climbed out of the Suburban.

"Over here," called one of the members of Sam's team, stepping out of the vehicle he was driving, an old Chevy pickup truck.

When Brady ran over he saw Sam sitting in the passenger seat of the truck, holding onto a bloody shoulder.

"Doc!" Brady called and waved him over.

Sam said, "Have him look at the others first. I've got several wounded. I can hang on for a bit longer."

"What happened, Sam?"

"They laid low and ambushed us. They must have been monitoring our frequency and knew we were coming. One of them fired early, before we were in the kill zone, inside the compound fences. The rest jumped out and began firing. I saw one of them turn to the man that had fired first and shoot him in the back of the head. Everyone tried to turn around or back up and we just interfered with one another. But we finally got away from them. We maybe got one or two, but that's all. It was a mess. We stopped when we got out of range and swapped injured drivers for uninjured and headed for your place for help."

"We'll do what we can. Do you think they are on your tail?"

"I don't know. I don't think so."

Brady deployed his people in a hasty ambush just back up the road a little ways in a sharp turn. Drivers took the vehicles well clear and came back to join the ambush. Brady sent the doctor and his nurse with Sam's crew to Brady's compound while he commanded the rear guard action.

Brady waited until almost dark before calling off the ambush. They loaded up and hurried back to the compound. It wasn't good news when they got there. Three of the ten people Sam had with him had died. Three more had serious wounds, including Sam.

When Brady was able to talk Sam again, after he'd been seen to by the doctors, Brady got another shock. It hadn't come up in the first conversation. "I saw Harvey Blankenship and two other men I recognized. It was Colonel Machabee's group. They've gone rogue. I can't believe it of the Colonel. His group has been a big help every time they were needed."

"Don't blame the Colonel. He's dead. Tied up and slaughtered with two others. His men must have turned on him. There wasn't a scrap of food in the place, though even if they had left for some other reason, they would have taken it. Why wouldn't they have contacted us? We could have spared some food for them."

"Us too," Sam said.

Brady didn't want to bother him anymore. The pain killer that Doctor Amos had given Sam was taking effect. And Sam obviously didn't know any more than he'd stated.

Star came up to Brady. He was staring off into space, thinking. "Are you all right?" She asked, putting a hand on his shoulder.

"No. We don't need this. I mean, a nuclear war and Yellowstone. Survivors shouldn't be fighting survivors. It's just not right!"

"I know, Brady. But we have to deal with it."

"We will," Brady said coldly. "With a vengeance. Come on. I want to talk to the other MAG commanders."

It was the first time Star had ever seen Brady angry. He threw down the microphone and said a bad word. "I cannot believe the others refused to join us in an attack! Don't they realize we're all at risk until this situation is resolved? They've turned rogue and killed their own. They are liable to do anything. We have to stop them as quickly as possible."

"Do you think… what about the families?"

"I don't know," Brady looked glum. "This is not going to be simple. Would you go find Harry and Barbara? We need to brainstorm this. And check the security team. Make sure they are on high alert."

"Okay," Star got up and headed outdoors. Brady was depending more and more on her and she liked the feeling and the responsibility. After finding Harry and Barbara and sending them to see Brady, Star stopped at the MAG armory. She still carried her Walther in the inside the waistband, small of back holster, but she had taken to carrying one of the MAG's Glock 21's in a flap holster on her hip. Brady had checked her out on it before issuing it to her.

At her insistence, Brady had also trained her on everything else in the armory. She picked up a Steyr AUG from the armory and went to help the security detail. She joined the rovers on top of the wall, encouraging them and setting an example.

When Barbara and Harry showed up Brady took them and Dr. Amos to his housing unit for a private conference.

"What is your take on this?" he asked, after filling them in on everything he knew about the situation.

"We have to address it quickly," Barbara said. "As much as I hate violence, I think violence is the only response to this."

"Me, too," Harry said. "We have to root them out and destroy them. I don't relish the idea of being on constant high alert, waiting for them to attack us."

Dr. Amos didn't respond, just nodding his head in agreement.

"Something we haven't considered is the fate of those in the Lowry compound. Did they kill them all, or are they holding them?" Brady asked. "We very well may be risking innocent lives if we attack."

"That place won't sustain a double population," Harry replied. "The Lowery MAG was scraping by as it was."

"You think we might be able to infiltrate and scout the situation?" Harry asked.

Brady shook his head. "They are almost all ex-military. I'm sure they are on alert now that what they've done is known. That fact is also going to make it difficult to attack successfully, without losing a lot of people."

"I just don't know," Barbara said her voice low. "I really don't want to make this kind of decision, Brady. The survival aspects were okay. Some hard decisions had to be made, but this... A lot of people are going to die, no matter what we do."

"I'll back you, Brady," Harry said, "Whatever you decide."

"Ditto," Dr. Amos said.

Their words were leaving the decision totally up to Brady and Brady knew it. "There is something bothering me about the Machabee compound," Brady said after a long silence. "I want to check it out before I make a decision."

The trio broke up and Brady went to the armory and then to the Suburban, ordered the gates open, and left the compound. Star saw the vehicle leaving and ran down to find out where Brady was going.

"He shouldn't be going off by himself in a situation like this!" she protested, more concerned than she wanted to admit. She was ready to go after him in another vehicle, but Barbara and Harry talked her out of it, insisting that Brady would be more upset if they let her go than if he ran into trouble.

Brady took his time going back to the Machabee compound, not expecting an ambush, but too cautious not to take precautions. He made it to the compound without a problem. He parked the Suburban and got out, carrying an HK-91. He kept it at the ready as he wandered around the compound, searching for he didn't know what.

Despite his care the voice from the edge of the forest caught him by surprise. "Turn around and put down your weapons! I have you in my sights!" It was a woman's voice. It sounded scared, but firm.

Brady hesitated but the unmistakable sound of a pump shotgun racking convinced him. He laid the HK-91 down and then took the Glock 21 from its holster and put it down beside the HK.

"Turn around, too," came the voice.

Brady did so, his hands out to his sides. She hadn't told him to put them up. He tensed when he heard running footstep coming toward him. "Take two steps forward and stop."

Brady didn't move. When he felt something prod him in the back he spun, knocking the barrel of the shotgun out of line with his body, continuing the spin with a low sweeping kick. His booted foot caught the woman in the ankles and she went down hard, the shotgun flying away.

When he stopped the turn and spun back around he suddenly realized that it was no woman, but a mere girl child. She couldn't have been more than twelve or thirteen. She was huddled on the ground now, crying, her long blonde hair hanging down over her face.

"Geez!" Brady whispered, going to one knee to try to comfort her. "I'm not going to hurt you," he said, reaching out to touch her shoulder. She shied back away from him.

"What is your name?" he asked gently, not trying to touch her again.

"You know who I am! You're one of them!"

"Them? The people from this compound?"

"Yes."

"I'm not. I'm Brady. From the St. Louis MAG compound. Are you hurt? Can you stand up?"

"Really? You're not one of them?"

"Honest. I won't hurt you."

The girl didn't protest as Brady helped her to her feet. She took a step and almost fell. "Ow! My ankle!"

Brady went to one knee. He felt of her ankle. It wasn't broken, but he'd obviously bruised her badly when he kicked her feet out from under her.

"I'm sorry," Brady said, standing up again. "I didn't know."

She didn't comment about the ankle, instead asking, "Do you have any food?"

It was her turn to tense when Brady leaned down and picked up his weapons. He holstered the Glock, and slung the HK. He stepped over and picked up the shotgun. It was a Remington .410 bore 870 pump. He handed it to her.

Her eyes got big. "You're giving it back to me?"

"Yes. I want you to know you can trust me."

"It's empty," she said.

"What? You braced me with an empty shotgun?"

"Uh-huh."

"Come on over to the truck. I have some jerky and gorp."

She was limping, but she followed Brady to the Suburban. He handed her the food and a canteen of water. She was tearing the jerky with her teeth, barely taking time to chew it. Brady stood silently, letting the obviously starving girl eat until she finally stopped and took a drink of water. "Thanks. I was starving. Can I keep this for later?"

Brady nodded. "Can you tell me what your story is?" His eyes kept scanning the forest and the entry into the compound, as she began to talk.

"We got really low on food."

Surprised, Brady asked, "You're a member of the group?"

She frowned. "Not anymore! Not after what they did!"

"What is your name?"

"Claudia Machabee. Colonel Machabee was my Uncle."

"Okay, Claudia, go on."

"We got really low on food. They stopped feeding the ones that got sick during the winter and just let them die. Uncle Bob was against it, but Captain Meyers forced him to let it happen. Uncle Bob wasn't the same after Aunt Jean died. Before he was really powerful. But he just couldn't seem to tell people what to do after she died from food poisoning.

"Captain Meyers said it was your fault she died. Because you wouldn't send a doctor to help her when she was sick."

"What? We never got a call about anyone sick here!"

"Really? I bet Captain Meyers was lying about it. I caught him in a bunch of lies, but Uncle Bob wouldn't believe me. Captain Meyers kept talking bad about your group. He scouted the place out he said and you guys were taking stuff from the other groups."

Brady just shook his head. This Captain Meyers sounded like a head case.

"When it got really bad, Uncle Bob and a couple of the others stopped eating almost completely and began insisting we get help. He ordered Captain Meyers to contact you, but the Captain said you wouldn't answer. That you were just waiting until we died to come take our stuff. I don't know why Uncle Bob didn't get on the radio himself to check, but he didn't. He believed in the chain of command, he said. I don't really know what he meant, but he wouldn't do anything about Captain Meyers. I hate him!" Claudia's eyes blazed. "He tried to do stuff with me, but I wouldn't let him."

"Where were your mother and father?" Brady asked.

Her face fell. "They sent me down here with Uncle Bob and Aunt Jean. They never got here."

"I'm sorry," Brady said gently. "Can you go on?"

Claudia nodded, sniffing back tears. "They tried hunting, but they said not much game survived. And Captain Meyers and some of them started talking about eating someone when they died. There were big arguments. I wasn't supposed to hear them, but I did. Uncle Bob seemed to come alive. He was really mad. Then a few days ago one of the babies died and some of them were going to cook it and eat it. That's when... I don't know the word... Captain Meyers said he was taking over. They tied up Uncle Bob, Captain Murcheson, and Emily Waters. They were good friends with Uncle Bob and helped out a lot.

"A bunch of the women tried to stop the men from cutting up the body. Captain Meyers was looking at me funny. I guess I went kind of crazy. I sneaked into the gun room and got my shotgun and ran away and hid in the woods. My dad and uncle used to take me camping all the time. I can shoot good, but I was scared and forgot to take extra shells for the shotgun.

"Some men came after me, but I've been out in the woods a bunch, trying to hunt squirrels and rabbits the way

Daddy taught me. I knew lots of places to hide. They quit looking after a couple of days, after I shot one of them. I don't think I killed him because he was really cussing and screaming.

"I kept sneaking back close then, hoping I could run in and let Uncle Bob and the others go, but I couldn't." Claudia started to cry softly then, but continued with her story. "Then they brought them out and all the guys and some of the girls all shot them at once. Then they all got into the trucks and left. Some of the women didn't want to go, but the others made them. I didn't know what to do so I just hid in the woods. I was here getting water when the trucks came. I thought they'd come back, so I hid deeper in the woods. I guess it was you guys. I wish I'd come out then."

"So that is why the generator was running. I couldn't figure that out."

Claudia nodded. She didn't struggle when Brady took her in his arms and let her cry for a long time. Finally, when even the sobs had stopped, Brady put her in the Suburban and headed back to the compound.

When Star saw the Suburban coming up the road in the near darkness she hurried down to the gate. But she waited until Brady gave the password and she gave the countersign before she opened the gates to let him in.

She stared open mouthed when she saw Claudia sitting in the front passenger seat of the Suburban. Hastily she closed the gates and then ran over to the Suburban. "This is Claudia," Brady said. "Would you get her some fresh food and help her clean up? Have Dr. Amos take a look at her, too."

"Come on, Claudia," Star said, taking Claudia's free hand in hers. Claudia clutched the shotgun, and the bags of jerky and gorp in the other. "My name is Star."

"Hi, Star. Cool gun," Claudia said, looking at the AUG.

Star's eyes met Brady's, but he just shrugged. She led Claudia off toward the women's dorm unit. She notified the rest of the security crew that she was off the wall and would be for some time.

Barbara and Harry, as well as several others, came up as Brady headed for the community building.

Brady told the others they would be filled in later, and took Barbara and Harry to his housing unit for another private conference. After he'd related Claudia's tale to them Harry said, "Jiminy Cricket! That's all we need! Cannibals! I only thought that was in the pre-war fiction."

Barbara looked sick. "A baby? I can't believe it."

"She has no reason to be lying," Brady said. "I believe her."

"Oh, I believe it. I just don't believe it."

"You think some of the other MAG's will help us now, if we tell them about this?" Harry asked.

"I guess it's worth a try," Brady said. "I'll contact them in the morning and try. We have to get on this quick. I don't think that group will wait around long before they attack. Apparently the new leader has some kind of grudge against either the MAG, me, or both."

"What was his name again?" Barbara asked.

"Captain Meyers," Brady said. "Claudia didn't use his first name."

"That rings a bell," Barbara said slowly. "Let me check the records over at the MAG office."

"Okay. I'd better fill in the others."

The three went about their tasks. There was an uproar when Brady mentioned the cannibalism to the group gathered in the community meeting room.

Star came up to Brady after the news had been passed. "I've got her in the room next to mine," she said. "The Doc said she's fine. Just malnourished. I'll make sure she gets enough good food to get her back up to par."

"Thanks, Star."

Barbara and Harry both came up to them at the same time. "I knew I'd heard the name," Barbara said, glancing around to make sure no one else was close. Edward Kent tried to sponsor him. Meyers wanted to bring several people in with him to be our 'Security Force', quote, unquote. You nixed the idea immediately. Kent got mad and pulled out of the MAG. That was early on."

"Don't recall it at all," Brady said. "I'll take your word for it."

"I've been quizzing everyone that helps with security patrols," Harry said. "There have been reports of 'maybe' seeing someone in the woods, but every time a recon patrol went out, they found nothing at all."

"Was probably Meyers or some of his people. I remember the reports. I laid it off to over-cautiousness. Should have taken it more seriously. That gives me a real sense of urgency, now," Brady said. "If they've scouted us, they might very well attack much sooner than I first thought they might. I really hope the other MAG's are willing to send people when I talk to them in the morning. For now I want to try to get some sleep."

The group went their own way, with Brady headed for bed.

It was just past 4:00 AM when the alarm came over the speaker on Brady's bedside table. Brady hastily dressed, grabbed his weapons and headed outside. The primary investors housing units were essentially soundproof. Brady didn't hear the gunfire until he got outside.

He headed for the parapet walls at a dead run, the musette bag of spare magazines for the HK banging at his side. He reached the closest stairs just behind Star. She was carrying an AUG and wore a chest harness for her spare magazines.

The leader of the security patrol ran crouched over to join them. The three knelt behind the parapet wall and Tom Kieroff filled Brady and Star in. "Got them all around us now. They rammed the gates with a deuce and a half, under cover of sniper fire. I think most of the group was right behind the truck, expecting it to breach the gates. We got the flood lights on and took a pretty good toll as they were running for cover. Now they've spread out and are sniping from the trees all around."

"Get Drusilla up here with her Barrett. They may have concealment, but they won't have cover behind a tree from that .50 BMG of hers. Star, have whoever is on comms to alert the other MAG's and see if any of them will send a force to attack from the rear. And then get more night vision goggles and hand them out as people man the walls. We'll kill the lights when Drusilla is set so she can use the night vision scope."

Crouching, Star ran for the stairs, and Tom went to get Drusilla. It was only moments later that Drusilla showed up on her own, carrying the heavy Barrett Model 82A1. She, like Brady, favored a musette bag for spare magazines.

Tom directed her to where the greatest fire was coming from. The team that had been on sentry duty put their night vision goggles back on and covered the lenses until Brady gave the signal to kill the lights. As soon as the lights died, those around Drusilla set up a heavy covering fire while she took aim through the night vision scope.

Ten quick shots later and most of the incoming firing stopped, all around the compound. Drusilla ducked down and changed magazines. "Got four KIA for sure," she told Brady, "and three probable's. Don't know about the other three rounds. Might have, might not."

"Okay. Good work. Change positions and let the others spot targets for you. Don't do more than two or three rounds at a time before you move."

"Don't worry," Drusilla said. "I'm not making more of a target of myself than I have to."

Brady let her and Tom do their stuff. He circled around and took the night vision goggles Star handed to him. She followed along as he headed for the gates. Tom had said they hadn't been breached but he wanted to check for vulnerability there anyway.

Satisfied the gates would continue to keep out the intruders, he and Star went back up to the parapet wall and added their fire to their companions'. The fire from the woods had slackened considerably. They heard a whistle blast three times, and then three times more. The incoming fire ceased.

Drusilla continued to fire several more times, at the greenish figures scampering too close to the edge of the woods, heading for their recall point. When headlights flared down the entrance road, Drusilla and Tom, carrying the Barrett between them ran for the ramparts by the gate.

Quickly inserting a new magazine, Drusilla began firing a pattern toward the vehicle lights. Engines roared and the lights danced. Two vehicles were still sitting, lights on, when the others disappeared down the road.

The lights were turned back on and the compound stayed on full alert the rest of the night. When they had full daylight, a recon team was sent out wearing body armor, led by Tom. They maintained constant radio contact with Brady and the rescue force that was ready to go after them if they ran into trouble.

"No sign of anyone around," Tom radioed in. "Expect for the bodies, of course. Haven't found any injured. Man, you should see what that Barrett does to a body. And trees. At least one of the guys was killed from the splinters spalled out of the back side of the tree he was trying to hide behind."

When the group came back in, Tom went over to Drusilla, who was standing by with the Barrett. "Did you have to hole the blocks in those two trucks? We could have used them."

Drusilla just patted the receiver of the Barrett and said, "Sweet Sue here does what Sweet Sue does."

With the way apparently clear, Brady dispatched the recon team out again to accompany two people in the Toolcat 5600T with a trailer to recover the nineteen bodies and gear of the slain. After that they took one of the U500 Unimogs and moved the deuce and a half, as well as the two dead vehicles up to the outside parking lot.

Dr. Amos reported to Brady shortly after that. No one in the compound had been killed, but three were seriously wounded, and six others had minor wounds. "Everyone should make it, except Dandy Two-Step. He's iffy. He's in a coma now. Only time will tell. We'll do what we can. There just isn't much we can do with a serious head injury."

Brady nodded. They'd paid a price. So had the enemy. The loss of nineteen people had to have decimated their force, even if some of the Lowery group joined forces with Meyers. He didn't want to wait to allow them to regroup. Brady decided they would go after Meyers and the group at the Lowery compound two days hence.

But they didn't have to attack. Around noon the next day, a man came up the road waving a white flag. He was under the muzzles of half a dozen rifles the entire time. "Captain Meyers' wants a parley," he called up to those behind the parapets by the gates.

Brady was sent for. The man waited nervously until Brady showed up at the parapet. "Tell Meyers to come in with his hands up and empty, along with all his people. We'll talk then."

"Won't do it. Look. He told me to negotiate for him if you wouldn't agree to talk to him."

"Nothing to negotiate," Brady said. "Unconditional surrender or open war."

"At least let me in to talk to you about it."

"Bring him in," Brady said, and headed down to the gate.

Through a spy hole, Tom told the man to take off all his clothes down to his shorts. The man began to curse Tom, but Tom calmly said, "It's that or no entry."

Star finally got to see the purpose of the pipe sticking out of the gate. Tom unlatched and pulled free the heavy assembly that plugged the outside of the pipe. He also slid back the cover to an opening on the top of the pipe, about in the middle of the projecting pipe. Star hadn't noticed it before.

"Crawl in," Tom told the man. There was more cussing, but the man did so, yelping at the coolness of the pipe on his bare skin.

Brady was standing by the opening of the pipe. He had his Glock 21 in hand. When the man's head showed in the opening, Brady put the barrel of the Glock against the back of the man's head. "Stop," Brady said. "Listen carefully. You do anything at all stupid you will be shot. Now state your business."

The man cursed loud and long, but he didn't move. Brady held the Glock steady on the back of the man's head. "The captain wants food for twenty people for a month, some ammo, and gas. We'll leave the area and leave you alone if you do."

"And if we don't?"

"He'll start killing hostages. The Lowery women and children."

"Brady!" one of the sentries. "There's two more out there. A man and a woman. The guy is holding a gun to the head of the woman."

"Go tell the madman we'll do it." There were protests all around Brady, but he waved them away. "Go," he said again and removed the gun from the man's head. The man quickly dressed and ran down the road. He passed the man and woman and cut into the woods.

Brady turned to Tom. "Out the tunnels. No mercy." Tom ran off.

Brady went back up behind the parapet. "You got a shot, Drusilla?" he asked. She was behind the parapet wall now with the Barrett. She had it sighted in on the man holding the gun on the woman.

"Oh, yeah. He's dead meat you give the word."

From the forest came an amplified voice. "You're making the right choice, Collingsworth. And just to show you how serious we are…"

When the voice began to fade Brady yelled to Drusilla. "Take him!"

The Barrett sounded and the man fell before he could pull the trigger. But it didn't save the woman. A dozen shots rang out from the forest behind her. She fell dead before she could take a step.

"Don't do that again!" Brady yelled toward the forest. "We're getting things ready right now! Give us time!"

Another man and woman stepped out into view. This time the man stayed right behind the woman, a gun to her head as well.

Again the amplified voice rang out. "You have fifteen minutes. If I don't see those gates open I'll kill a hostage every minute until they are."

"Geez!" Brady barely breathed. "Hurry Tom," he added, also under his breath.

Less than a minute before the time limit shots began to ring out in the forest. The man holding the gun on the woman moved just enough for Drusilla to take him out. The woman fell to the ground. Brady couldn't tell if she'd been shot or dropped on her own. He had his HK up and ready and when several people tried to cross the road to get away from part of Tom's attacking force they were caught in the road and slaughtered from behind, from in front by the other half of Tom's force, and from the side from the parapets.

Another group of armed and armored people stood ready at the gates. Brady gave the word and the gates opened just enough to let them out. They spread out and ran, zigzagging as they did so, to join the fight already in progress. In less than ten minutes it was over. Tom called Brady on the radio and Brady went out to join him.

Tom was standing near a man with his hands tied behind his back, under the close guard of two of Tom's people. "This him?" Brady asked.

When Tom nodded Brady pointed the HK at him, but after a few moments of hesitation, let the muzzle drop. "There'll be a trial," Brady said. "You'll get a chance you didn't give these other people."

"No, there won't," Meyers said and lunged at Brady. The two guards both fired. Meyers' forehead bounced off Brady's boots.

"What about the others?" Brady asked.

"I don't think anyone else survived. I'll go check."

"What about the hostages?"

"See for yourself," Tom said, pointing to spot at the edge of the road. Brady went over and stepped passed the first couple of trees, coming into a small open area. Some of Tom's men were standing around the perimeter, but not interfering in what was going on.

The Lowery women were taking vengeance on the women from the Machabee group for the deaths of their men, and the treatment they'd received from them. There were cries for help and for mercy, but Brady turned around and left. The world could be a cruel place.

When it was all sorted out only one of the Machabee women survived. She had at least tried to help those at the Lowery compound. The Machabee children had been spared. Brady's MAG took most of the Lowery women and children in, as well as the Machabee children. A few opted to go to Sam's compound, when the offer was made. The Machabee woman worked out a deal with Juan and his wife to stay with them and work in trade for room and board.

CHAPTER EIGHT

It was another short growing season, but enough food crops and fuel crops were produced and processed to allow all the remaining compounds to survive another winter. Which was as bad or worse than the previous one. One of the few services the federal government had resumed was the National Weather Service. Anyone with shortwave capability could get regional forecasts. The forecasts were broadcast twice a day on the Time Standard frequencies. The long range forecasts were calling for continued cool summers and savage winters for at least four more years.

There was talk of trying to relocate the MAG further south to avoid the worst of the weather. Brady was ambivalent about it, sometimes agreeing and sometimes not. The decision was put off for another year. Game was beginning to come back into the area, and there was much new growth of vegetation. Brady was careful to only let the firewood team cut deadwood. There was quite a bit of it from the radiation and the ash fall. He wanted every living thing to continue that could. The volcanic ash was already breaking down, enriching the soil where it had accumulated.

Star and her new shadow, Claudia, were at Brady's housing unit helping him do a spring cleaning. He'd always been a neat housekeeper, but so much of his time was taken up with MAG business he had let the housekeeping go.

Claudia and Star were on each side of Brady's bed, making it up. Claudia didn't see the wistful look on Star's face, as she looked over at Brady, putting clothing away in the closet, and then looked at the bed again, as she carefully smoothed the coverlet.

All three felt the sudden tremor shake the place. And all three ran out into the open, not so much for safety since the construction had stood up well to the earthquakes related to the Yellowstone super eruption, as to get to the communications station and find out what was going on.

As they ran toward the blast shelter Star asked, "You think it's Yellowstone again?"

"Different feel," Brady replied, going down the steps to the shelter. "What do you have, Connie?"

"Reports just now coming in, Boss. Looks like it's some of the New Madrid earthquake zone letting loose."

"Might not be too bad, then," Brady said. "It acts up every once in a while. Let's just hope it's not the 'Big One'."

"Don't tempt fate," Star said.

Another tremor rocked them on their feet.

"See," Star said.

"Still small," Brady said.

More people were coming into the shelter, looking for news. Brady told them what he knew for the moment, and then sat down beside Connie to monitor the situation. Star and Claudia went back to Brady's housing unit. "What do you say we make him a pan of brownies?" Star asked.

Claudia's eyes lit up. "Yeah! He'd like that!"

Star ruffled Claudia's hair. "So would you, wouldn't you?"

Claudia smiled at her substitute mom. "Yeah. I guess so."

"Me, too." Star led the way into Brady's kitchen. She'd rearranged it herself that morning so she knew where everything was.

Brady hadn't come back by supper time, so, with a little smile on her face, while Claudia studied her schoolwork, Star fixed them a supper. Brady came in the door just as she put things on the kitchen table.

He sniffed the air as he came toward the kitchen. "Hey! What's going on?"

"I thought you might be hungry, it being supper time," Star said. "What news do you have?" she asked.

"Definitely the New Madrid Earthquake Zone. Both shakes were felt in a wide area. Wow! This looks and smells good. I didn't even know you could cook."

"I've been helping in the community kitchen some when I'm not busy elsewhere."

"You're always busy, it seems like," said Claudia, putting her books away.

"Wash your hands," Star reminded her.

Claudia did so at the kitchen sink, and Brady did likewise. He moved to seat Star when she started to sit down. "Oh. Thank you."

Grinning, Claudia waited until Brady moved to her chair.

"See, Claudia," Star said, "Manners aren't dead."

Brady took his seat and reached for the entrée. "May I say Grace?" Claudia suddenly asked.

Bringing his hand back to his lap, Brady said, "Yes, Claudia, of course." He looked over at Star and saw that her eyes had misted over.

Claudia thanked God, and Jesus, and Star, and Brady.

After she said Grace, Claudia immediately reached for the biscuits. "My Mom used to make biscuits all the time. They're my favorite. Biscuits and rabbit stew. It's the best."

"Really," Brady asked. "Well, the animals are coming back. Maybe I can get us one or two if Star agrees to cook them." He looked over at Star. So did Claudia.

"Will you, Star?"

"Sure I will. I never have, but if you help me I'm sure I can do it."

"I used to help Mom all the time." She turned to Brady. "Can I go with you to hunt? I'm pretty good. I've shot rabbits before."

"I believe you told me that before. Sure."

"Could we make it a threesome?" Star asked.

"I don't see why not. And if you don't mind, I'd like to shoot your vierling."

"What's that?" asked Claudia, after swallowing a large bite of biscuit.

The conversation turned to guns and shooting and hunting and fishing. Claudia held up more than her end of the conversation, as she seemed the much more experienced of the three. The closest Star had come to hunting was shooting skeet with her father. Brady had only hunted a few times, at the invitation of a couple of his employees who hunted.

It was Brady that suggested they watch a movie after their dinner. Claudia and Brady helped Star clean up and do the dishes. They took their brownies and milk to the living room and discussed a movie from Brady's collection of DVD's.

Claudia was sitting between Star and Brady on the sofa. She fell asleep almost immediately. Brady fell asleep soon after. Star got up quietly and eased an afghan over the two, and then sat back down to watch the end of the movie.

She shook Brady gently after the movie ended. "Brady," she whispered. "Wake up. Movie is over. Brady." She shook him again. He came to with a start.

"Oh. Movie is over? I guess I fell asleep."

"I'll say," Star replied, still speaking softly. "I need to get Claudia up and off to bed."

"Oh. Sure." After a moment's hesitation Brady said, "I hate to wake her. Why don't we just put her to bed in the second bedroom?"

Star nodded and removed the Afghan and Brady picked up Claudia. He carried her to the second small bedroom and left Star with her to get Claudia in bed. He gathered up the brownie plates and milk glasses and rinsed them in the sink in the kitchen.

When he went back to check on them Star was standing in the doorway of the bedroom, watching Claudia. "She never even woke up," Star told Brady, her voice very low.

"Brady," she said then, stepping right up to him. He leaned back against the door jam. "I want to stay, too. With you." She leaned forward slightly more and her lithe form molded to his. She kissed him gently on the lips and then again more firmly.

Brady responded to the second kiss, kissing Star deeply, his hands going to her back. He took her hand then and led her to his bedroom.

The next day she moved her things and Claudia's things into Brady's place. They were a family now.

CHAPTER NINE

The tremors didn't stop. They had shock after shock during the winter, sometimes two or three a day. Brady read up on the history of the New Madrid Earthquake Zone. He didn't like what he found out. There had been a whole series of moderate quakes leading up to several big ones during 1811 and 1812. The pattern seemed to be repeating itself.

From what the amateur operators were telling him the world was acting up geologically all over. Yellowstone had blown and The Pacific Rim was alive with erupting volcanoes now. Some had been active, but many dormant ones were becoming active again. There were even reports of some new fissures opening up and creating new cones in several areas.

The material going into the atmosphere from the volcanoes was one reason the National Weather Service kept pushing back the timeframe for the climate to return to a more 'normal' set of seasons.

Brady, Star, and Claudia were working in their section of the garden when the world around them seemed to go wild. Noise beyond what one could imagine sounded and the very ground dropped from beneath their feet. Claudia screamed and Brady and Star both tried to grab her but all three fell to the ground when the ground itself stopped falling.

Brady had no reference of how far the ground had subsided, but he felt like he had fallen several feet.

It was generations before scientists pieced together what had happened that day and several subsequent days. A tectonic movement of epic proportions had snapped the North American Tectonic Plate in two from deep in the Gulf of Mexico up the Mississippi River Valley and over to the Great Lakes and the St. Lawrence Seaway.

For eons the bedrock deep under the center of the United States had been stretched thinner and thinner, resulting in the Reelfoot Rift. The surface would have sunk with the bedrock, except billions of tons of eroded rock coming from the Rockies and the Appalachians, and even the Ozarks, had filled the sunken land in, just slightly slower than the ground was sinking.

When the plate separated magma began to stream upward in hundreds of places. But it was still deep in the earth and much of it cooled and hardened quickly, sealing the crack except for here and there. A new line of volcanoes arose along the length of the split.

The waters of the Gulf of Mexico flowed northward over the sunken ground, stopping only when it reached Cape Girardeau, Missouri in the north, the Ozarks in the west, and the foothills of the Appalachians to the east. The Gulf of Mexico was now the American Sea.

Water flowed from the Atlantic into the new sea, and the Pacific flowed into the Atlantic. It took years for the oceans to equalize. In that time old currents disappeared and new ones were created.

The tremors continued for days. Communications were out. Brady and his group, and the other groups close, had no idea of the extent of what was happening. They only knew that the greatest earthquakes in recorded history had occurred. And they had survived them. So far. There was doubt in some minds about their future survival. One thing they noticed and couldn't explain was the occasional scent in the air much like that of the sea.

They also couldn't explain the loss of so many Amateur Radio contacts along the Gulf Coast. At first. Then the reports started to come in. Brady and the others found out they were only a few miles from the new coastline.

But life in the Ozarks went on for another year. There had been marriages and births and some additional deaths. Some of the marriages were between residents of different compounds. One of the births was Star and Brady's son, Joshua Brady, named after Star's father and Brady.

But the Ozarks had become a very small gene pool. There was pressure to go exploring and find some of the other survivors they talked to on the radio. Also to set up a presence on the new coast to take advantage of the bounty of the sea. So Brady's MAG, in cooperation with the other Ozark locals, set up a plan to go to the nearest coast.

But that is a story for another time.

131

OZARK RETREAT: PART TWO
PROLOGUE

"I don't know, Sweetie," Joshua Hardcastle said. "With things going the way they are, I don't think going on a world cruise is such a good idea."

"It's because of Precious, isn't it?" She used Joshua's daughter's name almost like a curse. "She's a spoiled little brat and you shouldn't cave in to her the way you do. She should be making a living for herself, not living off you."

"Of course Sue Billingsly living off me is all right," Joshua thought, but didn't say. "I like it this way. She's the only family I have or am likely to have." Sue had told him that outright. No babies.

"You have me," Sue said, slithering over to him and plastering her body against his. "Don't I keep you happy?"

"You do. You do," he said. And thought, "In bed."

"Let's wait until Precious gets here. Maybe she'll want to go. I feel bad about what happened the other day."

Sue un-plastered herself from her Sugar Daddy. A conniving frown curled her lips. "We need to leave tomorrow to get on the cruise. You believe me, don't you? She's the one that did it."

"Of course I do, Sweetie. Of course." Of course he'd never known Precious to lie to him, either. They couldn't both be telling the truth.

Sue used her best weapon. She took Joshua's hand and tugged. "Let's go upstairs. I'm in the mood."

It was too good an offer to refuse. Joshua went along eagerly.

While Joshua was napping afterwards, Sue got on the computer in the bedroom. She took his wallet from his pants and pulled out the Platinum American Express card. It took only moments to finalize the booking on the cruise, with payment in full. She'd been planning this for weeks after she found out the cruise was getting cancellations and bookings were again available. The bags were all packed, stored in a spare bedroom, without Joshua's knowledge.

CHAPTER ONE

Joshua couldn't bring himself to tell his daughter he was leaving, until he was leaving. As the Cruise Ship Elite left New York Harbor, he used his cellular phone to call her before they got out of range. Sue was suddenly no longer in evidence.

"Hi, Precious. I have something to tell you. I'm going on a world cruise with Sue.

"We're leaving the port now. Sue and I think you need some time away from me. To do more on your own. I know you can do it. You've done it at times before. Don't be mad, but I'm closing up the house, too, so you'll have to use your apartment. I put a hundred thousand in your credit card account, so you have plenty of money. And don't worry about us. Sue thinks this will all blow over, just like always. Bye."

Sue was back at his side. "How'd she take it?" she asked.

"Very well, actually," Joshua said, putting away the cell phone. He noticed that Sue seemed to be disappointed.

But she took his arm and said, "Let's go down and wait for them to open the casino."

With a sigh, Joshua went with her. He wasn't too interested in the casino. He'd gambled in most of the major casinos in the world. He'd never won big and he'd never lost big. It just really didn't intrest him much anymore. But the casino wasn't going to open until after the Lifeboat drill, anyway. They went to their suite and waited for the alarm to sound.

After the drill, Joshua left Sue, a glass of champagne in her hand, at the casino, that excited look in her eye of a gambling addict. She had several addictions, including alcohol. Joshua set about learning his way about the ship. He didn't like not knowing where everything was. When it was time for their early dinner seating Joshua had to go get her from the casino. She was already moderately drunk.

Joshua got her to the dining room and as much of a meal into her as he could. They were sitting facing the stern of the ship. Suddenly bright lights began to flare in the far distance. "Fireworks for us! Cool!" said Sue.

Absolute quiet fell over the dining room. But it didn't last. There was total pandemonium as people realized they were watching the nuclear destruction of New York and surrounding areas. Bells began to ring and then the Captain's voice came over the public address system.

"Be calm. Everyone go back to your staterooms while we find out what is going on. I assure you we are in no immediate danger. Go back to your staterooms. The crew will assist you if you cannot locate your stateroom. I will be talking to you again soon."

Joshua got Sue up on her feet. She was drunk. He half carried her toward the stateroom. He had to struggle slightly. She wanted to go back to the casino. "It's closed, Sue! We're at war now. Please. Please. Just let me get you to the stateroom."

"You're no fun," she said, but quit struggling. She seemed to have no grasp as to what had happened. As he started to undress her she tried to turn it into fun and games, but Joshua resisted the urge. He got her undressed and into bed. Hating to need to do it, he got a 50ml bottle of gin from the dispenser in the room and poured her a drink.

Joshua had been in the Navy, an ordinance tech on aircraft carriers. He knew the feeling of a ship suddenly accelerating and turning. They turned left slightly. They were now going almost due north rather than northeast.

Knowing better, Joshua tried to leave the suite. He was ushered back inside unceremoniously. He thought about unpacking the cases, but decided to wait until the Captain spoke again. Joshua checked on Sue. She was out, the empty glass lying on the bed beside her hand.

He took out a book and tried to read in the sitting room of the suite. Finally he just stood by the windows and stared out, thinking about Precious and how big a mistake he'd made.

The Captain didn't make them wait long. The alerting signal sounded and the public address system came alive again. "This is Captain Roger Bainseborough-Smith. It is my duty to inform you that a thermo-nuclear war has begun. The flashes of light we saw behind the ship were nuclear warheads detonating. Do not worry. We are steaming north by northeast at top speed to try and remove ourselves from the path of any fallout.

"I am going to allow you out of your staterooms now so you can use the facilities of the ship. Stay calm. Please do not go out onto the decks. You will be asked to return to your stateroom if you do so.

"If, in fact, we do begin to experience fallout you will be ordered to the lower levels of the ship. If such is announced, please cooperate with the crew. They will show you to the safest locations in the ship. Thank you. More later."

The Cruise Director came on and announced the various activities that would be available. Joshua wasn't interested in the activities. He wanted to know something. Figuring there would at least be some rumors floating around in the various bars on the ship; he left the out-for-the-night Sue and headed for the smoking parlor. He'd have a cigar and a tonic water and see if anyone knew anything else.

No one did, but there was plenty of speculation. Joshua discounted it all and just enjoyed his cigar. He didn't smoke often, but when he did, he enjoyed it. The cigar done, he headed back to the stateroom. Being among the obviously terrified passengers and crew of the ship was as bad as being in the suite. Quite a few of the passengers were getting drunk.

Joshua had an excellent sense of direction and took the shortest route to his suite. It led him past the children's arcade and play area. A rather harried looking woman in crew's uniform was chasing a laughing three or four year old child down the passageway. Another darted out of the play room. Joshua swept the little girl up and swung her in her arms the way he had done with Precious when she was little.

The little girl squealed in delight. The crewperson returned carrying her captive, who was not looking happy at the moment. Another female crewmember came hurrying up and took the girl from Joshua. "Thank you," the first woman told him.

He read her nameplate. Patricia Paine – Youth Activities Director "Looks like you have your hands full."

"Yes, we are quite busy. If you'll excuse me…" She hurried back into the play room and got the little boy involved in a toy before he began crying or screaming. There were a dozen children in the play room and at least that many older ones in the arcade. All of them seemed agitated.

"Feeling the tension of the adults," Joshua thought to himself.

Only Patricia and the other woman were in evidence. Another child headed for the door, but stopped and stared up at Joshua. Joshua guided him back to the toy box and helped him select a toy as Patricia arbitrated an argument in the Arcade.

It was midnight when the last child's parents stopped in to pick him up. Joshua had stayed the entire time, helping. Joshua was leaning against the door frame when Patricia came out of the Arcade with the teenage boy.

"Fallout yet, Dad?" he asked.

"No, son. Still no sign. Your mother and I have been keeping watch."

"Sure wish we could have brought our BOB's," he said as he followed his parents out into the passageway.

Patricia came up to Joshua and thanked him profusely for his help that evening. "Any time," Joshua replied. "Any time."

He went to the suite, undressed, and climbed into bed by Sue, wondering what the next few days would bring.

As beautiful as she could make herself, Sue was not a pretty morning person. She seldom let Joshua see her until she'd showered and had on makeup. It usually wasn't a difficult task. Joshua normally got up early and went for a run each morning. He was still in the suite when Sue woke up, groaning.

He went to the door of the bedroom of the suite and asked, "You okay this morning?"

"Yeah. Yeah. What happened last night?"

Joshua explained it to her. He wasn't sure she believed him, but she nodded and went to the bathroom. He went to the sitting room and waited for her. She took her usual hour to get ready. They were late for the dining room breakfast, but were able to get something at the buffet.

Watching the people moving around, Joshua decided many of them were in denial. The routine seemed normal for a cruise. It was the same with the crew. Most were acting as if nothing had happened. But as the day wore on, people began to talk. The Captain had not addressed the ship again.

The crew was still not letting anyone on deck. Sue asked for more casino money. He refused. Sue got an ugly look on her face, but it was gone in an instant. Joshua wasn't even sure if he'd seen it.

"Is it okay if I try the ATM? They have one, you know. I checked."

"Sure," Joshua responded. He didn't bother to tell her it wouldn't be working. "I couldn't get a run this morning. I'm going to get some exercise, walking the corridors. I'll meet you at the dining room for lunch."

"Whatever," Sue called over her shoulder, already headed for the ATM near the ship's bank. The card didn't work. She looked around to make sure Joshua wasn't anywhere around. She went to the bank counter and signed for cash on Joshua's shipboard account. She did have signatory power, so she got the money, no questions asked.

Joshua strolled firmly, corridor after corridor, staircase after staircase. He found himself at the Arcade and Children's play room. There weren't as many children about, but Patricia was busy with the ones that were. She smiled and waved at him. Joshua gave a smile and small wave back.

He stayed on that deck and made several circuits, stopping at the play room each time. Finally he had a chance to lend a hand. Patricia smiled her thanks and went to change one of the babies.

Joshua stayed there, helping with the children. Patricia had quit trying to get him to go along and let them deal with it, but more parents brought more children. Patricia admitted they were shorthanded. One of the crew in her department hadn't showed up for the cruise.

He left, reluctantly, to meet Sue for lunch. She was beaming, talking to a group of people about her own age. She ran over to Joshua when she saw him and wrapped her arm around his. "I won! Big! Almost a thousand dollars!"

She didn't tell him she'd spent twelve hundred to make the thousand.

Joshua was surprised. He'd been sure the ATM wouldn't work.

She was bubbly all through lunch, telling him about the people she'd met in the casino. They had invited her and Joshua to go dancing with them that evening after dinner. Joshua was disinclined, but Sue got him to agree the same way she usually did. Bedroom antics. Joshua had just stepped out of the shower, afterwards, when the public address system chime sounded and the voice of the Captain began speaking. Sue had already left the suite.

"Ladies and Gentlemen, this is the Captain speaking. I regret to inform you that my supposition that World War Three had begun last night has proven to be true. My communications officers have been trying to make radio contact all night into the morning. They were finally successful after the ionization of the atmosphere lessened.

"Both the United States and Europe have been devastated. Canada much less so. I have decided to make way for Canada after we get reports that the radiation that does exist on the eastern side of the nation has diminished. I assure you, we have enough provisions for a substantial wait. Over two weeks. There have been no signs of radioactive fallout. You may now use the regular outside decks. Please stay calm. The medical staff is available for those that may have problems dealing with this. More later."

Joshua dressed and headed for the open air. He breathed deeply, feeling more free than the situation warranted. He began to stroll the decks. There were many conversations about going to Canada, but he stayed out of them. He felt sorry for the Canadian citizens on board. They were being bombarded with questions.

He was going to go in and see if Patricia needed help in the Playroom, but ran into her on deck, supervising a group of youths playing shuffleboard. Joshua took a deck chair nearby and watched the children play. And Patricia. There was something about her, though Joshua couldn't define it. She wasn't stunningly beautiful the way Sue was, but she was very pretty. And carried herself very professionally.

She saw him finally and came over to thank him again for his help the night before and this morning. She had to go back to tend to the children. Joshua stayed and watched. He noticed a group gathering nearby and wandered over to see what was going on.

"I tell you they are!" said a woman, vehemently. "We have to do something about it."

Joshua had missed the first part of the conversation. He whispered to one of those on the perimeter of the small crowd. "What's going on?"

"She says the crew is beginning to lock people in their staterooms. People just wanting to find out what is going on."

Two ship's officers were approaching and Joshua saw the woman push through the small crowd and go up to them. They had to stop or run over her. "I demand to know why people are being locked up!"

"Madam," said one officer, "People are not being 'locked up'. There have been a few people restricted to their staterooms, but only on doctor's orders. Not everyone is handling this situation rationally. We are trying to keep panic down, and worry to a minimum. Just keep listening to the Captain's announcements. He will notify the passengers as new information comes in. Now if you will excuse me, I have duties to perform."

The woman didn't look happy as the two officers went around her and continued on their way.

"I figured as much," Joshua said to the man he'd asked about what was going on. "By the way, I'm Joshua Hardcastle."

"Jerry Bastigone. What do you think of all this war stuff? You think it's real?"

Joshua was shocked. How could the man not believe it was real? "I do believe it. I was sitting in the dining room and saw the explosions on the coast."

"Yeah. I know. Just wishful thinking on my part. What do you think the Captain will do?"

"I'm sure he is developing plans. I think going to Canada is a good start."

"I guess so. Have to make the best of it. Mostly I'm worried about my wife. She's not taking this well. I can't get her to come out of the stateroom. I just wish I knew what to do."

"Have the doctors' check on her. Maybe they can give her something."

"I think I will. Thanks. I'm kind of jittery, myself. You seem to be calm enough. That's a big help to me. I'll see you around. I'm going to go check on my wife."

Joshua nodded and decided he'd better go check on Sue. He tried the stateroom first, knowing the chance of finding her there was slim. She wasn't there. What was there, slid under the door, was the previous day's financial accounting summary. It was normal procedure for the cruise line to provide each passenger a summary of their purchases using the onboard credit system.

He found he wasn't that surprised when he saw the withdrawal from the deposit account. Sue was at it again. "I knew that ATM wouldn't work," he said aloud. He headed for the casino to find her, but he suddenly detoured to the ship's bank. He withdrew the entire deposit, except for one hundred dollars and then continued his journey to the casino.

"Oh, good!" Sue said, when Joshua went up to her at the roulette table. "Honey, I need a little more cash. I'm right on the verge of winning."

"Sue, Sweetie… I need to talk to you."

"But I'm so close!"

"Please, Sue."

Sue frowned but followed Joshua out of the casino. As soon as they were through the fancy double doors, Sue asked, "What is it, Sweetie? You in the mood again? That's okay. You know me. I'm always ready."

Joshua decided to let her think that. It would get her to the stateroom without a scene. She was already unzipping her skirt when Joshua unlocked the door to the stateroom.

"No, Sue. No. I didn't bring you down here for that. Not this time."

Sue let the skirt drop anyway. She'd always been able to manipulate him through sex. No reason she couldn't do it again.

"Sue. Stop that," he said, rather forcefully for him as Sue began to unbutton her blouse seductively.

Her hands dropped to her side, clinched into tiny fists. "What is it, Joshua?" Her anger was beginning to show through.

"It's your spending. Don't you understand what has happened? World War Three is raging right now. We're off on this cruise with nothing but the shirts on our backs. And a little money."

"You have plenty of money!" Sue laughed. "You're stinking rich!"

"Not any more, Sue. Don't you get it? My book wealth doesn't mean a thing now. I can't sell a few stocks to get you a new dress every week. All I have left is what I brought with me, and what is at the house, if it is even still there. Kansas City was probably a target. Money might not even be any good now. But as long as it is, we have to conserve what we have. It may come down to selling our jewelry."

"Like hell! I'm not selling anything! You gave those things to me. I won't let you take it back! If you can't take care of me, I'll just find someone that will!" Sue stormed out of the stateroom.

On a hunch, Joshua followed her, staying well behind. It was as he suspected. She'd headed straight to the ship's bank. Joshua watched her find out there was only a hundred dollars left in the deposit account. She was livid and began to curse. The bank clerk hurriedly gave her the hundred, to get her to quiet down, since she did have signatory powers. Joshua shook his head. Precious had been one-hundred-percent right about Sue. He'd been a fool not to listen to his daughter. Now he was stuck with her. It wouldn't be right to abandon her, as tempting as that would be.

He went to the ship's library and started researching Canada and possible routes to Kansas City. Precious was a resourceful young woman. There was an excellent chance she had survived. Joshua planned on finding her. He began to plan what he would do when they got to Canada.

One of his problems was solved, he discovered, when he went to dinner in the dining room. There was Sue, draped on the arm of an elderly gentleman, beaming and laughing with those around her as they went into the dining room together. Sue had found another Sugar Daddy.

The talk at the table he shared with three couples was all about what was to be done now that the world was at war. Joshua stayed mostly silent, speaking only when one of the others spoke directly to him.

The consensus was that the cruise line had an obligation to take care of everyone on the ship for the duration. It was all Joshua could do not bellow with laughter at the naïvety of the group.

After dinner Joshua went to the Smoking Parlor for a cigar. He ran into Jerry Bastigone having a cigarette. "How's your wife doing?" Joshua asked.

"Same. I tried to get her to go to the infirmary, but she refused. I don't know what to do. She can't stay in the stateroom forever. Going to have to quit these things. May not ever be a supply again."

Jerry lit another cigarette from the first one, belying his words. "What are you going to do when we get to Canada?" he asked Joshua.

"Head for Kansas City to find my daughter."

"You sound so certain. I don't have a clue what we will do. Try to settle down. I'm from New York. Not going to even think about going home. I'm sure I don't even have one, now. Probably have to go back to working with my hands to pay my way. Own... Owned a construction company, but it'll be back to hammer in one hand and nail in the other." When Joshua didn't comment, Jerry drifted away, leaving Joshua to his thoughts.

After his cigar, Joshua headed down to the Playroom and Arcade. Perhaps he could be of help again. There were only a couple of children, including the one young gentleman that had been the last to leave the other night. Joshua saw him in the Arcade. Patricia wasn't there. Since they weren't busy, she was taking a break. Disappointed, Joshua went out on deck. It was a bit cool this far north.

He took a turn around the deck. When he approached the stern of the ship he noticed their wake. It was curved. The ship was making a wide, sweeping turn, apparently heading for the Canadian coast line. Joshua went to the stateroom. Sue's belongings were gone, including her jewelry from the safe…so much for his responsibility for her welfare. She was now someone else's responsibility. Joshua undressed and went to bed, thanking his lucky stars he'd taken his own things from the safe after he'd discovered the spending summary.

CHAPTER TWO

Joshua went to the dining room for breakfast the next morning. There weren't that many eating in the dining room. The buffet had been busy when he passed it on his way down. Joshua started to take a bite of his Eggs Benedict when he heard something. He put down his fork. He knew that sound. It was a CF-18 buzzing the ship.

Like most of the others in the dining room he left his breakfast behind and went out on deck. A second CF-18, or more accurately, a CF-188, the Royal Canadian Air Force version of the F/A-18, flew by at ship's stack height.

The two aircraft joined up in formation, made a wide sweeping turn and came toward the ship from the side, well ahead of the bow. When they were close, the lead plane fired a burst from the 20mm cannon, which was part of its armament.

People screamed and dashed away from the bow as the aircraft cut across it. Joshua couldn't believe it. The Royal Canadian Air Force was warning them off. They weren't going to be allowed to disembark on Canadian soil.

The Captain confirmed Joshua's thought just after the jets took to a high altitude watch flight pattern. "Ladies and Gentlemen, I regret to inform you that we are not going to be allowed to make landfall on Canadian soil. A boat will be sent out for our Canadian passengers. They will be allowed to disembark the ship and go home. I will advise you of our next course of action soon. Stay calm and do not despair. We will find a safe place to put to shore."

There was pandemonium throughout the ship, passengers and crew alike. People were yelling epitaphs toward the unseen shoreline. Some people were just screaming. Others were crying. A few were trying to calm the others down.

Joshua turned and helped break up a fight. Two men had taken umbrage apparently with a Canadian passenger that was trying to defend Canada's actions. Members of the ship's crew rapidly hurried the Canadian away.

It was an hour before a Royal Canadian Navy patrol vessel rendezvoused with the motionless Elite. Many of the passengers and even some of the crew yelled more epitaphs and curses at those leaving the Elite and the crew of the patrol boat picking them up.

Joshua thought he was going to have to defend himself when he commented that he could understand why the Canadians were doing what they were doing. "Can't really blame them," he said. "Over two thousand people all in one place in the aftermath of a nuclear war? I don't think I'd want them coming to my home, either."

He made himself scarce as the ship began to move again. He wasn't about to get into a fist fight over his opinion. Joshua started to head for the Smoking Parlor, but shook his head. "Jerry is right about quitting smoking. He might as well give it up now as later. Instead of the Smoking Parlor he went to the library. Canada was out. The New England states were out unless he really missed his guess.

Hopefully the Captain would announce where they were headed soon. For the moment Joshua would do a little general research on the southeast coast of the US. He found what he could on the area and then went down for lunch.

Things had changed on the ship after the episode that morning. Joshua noticed it as soon as he left the library. People were talking in whispers, grim expression on their faces. There had been worry before, of course, but now it was worse. Before there was a safe destination in mind. Now there was only speculation.

Another change was the meal. Much more limited menu and the serving sizes were smaller for the most part. Passengers complained.

Some of the crew was becoming less polite and ready to please. More passengers complained. Joshua had a feeling the ship's officers were running into some employee relationship problems.

He had taken for granted the quick, courteous service of the officers and crew. Joshua quit doing that. He asked for little and expressed his thanks sincerely. He began tipping with ones for the little services he did get. He had a feeling that the crew might not be getting the accustomed tips at the end of the cruise. And that they knew it.

Joshua was right. There was full blown mutiny by dinner time. At least half the crew was refusing to work, from the looks of it. It was obvious in the dining room. The servers and bus people that were in evidence were covering twice or more their regular stations.

Many of the passengers made it worse, complaining to every crew member coming into earshot. Joshua noticed Sue and her new beau were some of the loudest of the bunch. Joshua quietly asked his server if there was some way he could help. She shook her head. "No, sir. Not now, anyway." She hurried off when someone at another table called for her loudly.

Joshua was at a loss. He went on deck after dinner, trying to sort possibilities in his head. They were traveling southeast now. Away from the North American Continent at an angle. Joshua assumed it was to avoid fallout and the ship would turn back to the west when the Captain was sure there was no more fallout. When he went to his stateroom he had to make up the bed.

He woke up to an announcement that the dining room was closed. The other various daily options for meals were being discontinued, as well. Meals would only be available at the buffet and portions would be limited. No seconds allowed.

When Joshua went up it was a mob scene. He saw Jerry standing in an out of the way corner, watching. There was a woman with him this time. Joshua noted her wan appearance, and jerky movements. Her eyes were never still, darting here and there as people moved about.

"Won't hurt me to miss a meal," Joshua said, patting his stomach, trying for a little levity.

"I've got to get June something to eat. She hasn't eaten anything since yesterday morning." Jerry turned appealing eyes to Joshua. "Would you wait here with her while I go try to get her something? She won't go up to the buffet with all the people there. I'm afraid they'll stop serving before she's willing to get something herself."

"Sure, Jerry. No worries." Joshua tried to engage June in conversation, but she just ignored him. She stepped behind him when someone came near them.

Jerry worked his way up the line and was able to come back some time later with a plate of food. "You'd better hurry," he told Joshua. "There's not much left and they said there won't be any more until dinner. No lunch." He took his wife over to a vacant table and sat down beside her. Joshua thought he was going to have to feed her, but she finally picked up the fork and began to eat.

When Joshua went over after the line had thinned out, he found that Jerry was right. There were only a few odds and ends left. He took what he could get, considering there wouldn't be anything until evening. Of course, there were still the items in the stateroom dispenser.

After he ate, Joshua tried to corral an officer to offer his assistance if they would take it. But they all seemed to be on missions of their own. He finally got one stopped long enough to make the offer. "Sir, the Captain will be addressing that issue this afternoon. Please wait until then and follow his lead."

"Will do," Joshua said. It sounded like the command crew was ready to let some of the passengers' help where they could.

That was exactly what the Captain announced. He didn't address the fact that some of the crew wasn't working, only that there had been offers of help from passengers and he would allow it in specific circumstances. People would need to keep up their staterooms on their own. That staff was needed elsewhere.

Joshua was one of the first ones to sign up. They put him to work with a vacuum cleaner, cleaning the common areas. The Captain was determined to keep the ship clean and orderly, Joshua decided. He finally noticed that he wasn't seeing any crew that wasn't working. He wondered where the mutineers were, but didn't ask.

Sue and her beau walked by and she laughed at him delightedly. "And to think I used to go out with you. I must have been out of my mind." She was still laughing as they walked away.

Though he hadn't expected it, Joshua found out there were a couple of perks for helping out. Those that worked that day were served meals in the crews mess. Nothing fancy or excessive, but a good, filling meal.

Jerry, when Joshua ran into him that evening, said it had been another mob scene at the buffet. June wasn't with him.

"Were you able to get June to eat again?"

With a sad smile on his face, Jerry shook his head. "Only what she ate this morning. I don't know what to do. She won't go see the doctor. I hate leaving her in the room by herself, but I just have to get out and get a cigarette every once in a while. I can't stand being in that stateroom for hours on end."

"I understand," Joshua told him. There wasn't much else to say. They each were lost in their own thoughts for a while and then Joshua said he was going down to his stateroom to go to bed.

"This early?" Jerry asked.

"Used muscles today I haven't used in years. I'm beat."

"You volunteered?"

"Yeah."

"I think I may do that tomorrow. For something to do."

"It would probably help. I'll see you tomorrow."

"Good night."

Joshua was up bright and early the next morning, having gone to bed as early as he had. He was a little sore and decided a run on the deck would be good for him. He made a couple of laps and then saw Jerry and June near the stern of the ship. Just before he turned to go to a stairway and go down and join them, he saw June say something to Jerry and Jerry leave.

When Joshua got down to the deck, he met Jerry coming out from inside the ship. "June wanted a cup of coffee. I was able to finagle one." Jerry looked around. "Where is she?"

"I don't know," Joshua said. They each walked toward opposite side of the ship to look down the length of the decks for her. "You see her over there?" Joshua called.

"No. You?"

Joshua shook his head. "Maybe she went back down to the cabin for a sweater. It is pretty cool out and I noticed she was wearing a sleeveless dress."

"Yeah. That's her favorite dress." Jerry handed Joshua the coffee. "I'm going to go check the stateroom."

A few minutes later he came running back, panic in his eyes. "We have to stop the ship! She's jumped!" He was waving a piece of paper. "She left a note! How do we stop the ship?"

Joshua ran to find an officer. Jerry was staring at the white wake of the ship. It was ten minutes before the ship began to slow and turn. Jerry ran to the furthest point he could go forward, and began to scan the ocean in front of them as the ship lined up with the wake.

Afraid Jerry would do something stupid, Joshua stayed right with him. A ship's officer came up to them and began to question Jerry about his wife. Jerry showed him the note. "She just couldn't handle what happened," he said. He was crying now. "She can't swim."

The Elite came to a stop and lowered several of the life boats to search a wider area and then the Elite began searching again, too. It was almost dark when the lifeboats were recalled. "I'm sorry, sir," said the officer. "We have to consider your wife lost at sea."

"No! Jerry groaned. He collapsed to his knees, sobbing. Joshua and the officer got him up and down to the infirmary. Joshua stayed in the infirmary while the doctor talked to Jerry and gave him something to calm him and help him sleep. Joshua walked him back to the stateroom, made sure he got into bed and then went up see if there was any food left from the buffet dinner. There wasn't.

Joshua got a can of nuts out of the self-serve dispenser in his stateroom and went to bed himself. He was exhausted mentally. Jerry's wife's suicide on top of the worry about his daughter was getting to him.

He went for a run on deck the following morning to work some more of the kinks out. Joshua noticed that their course was now to the southwest.

He was first in line for the breakfast buffet and then for the work details. It seemed to Joshua that there was a few more of the crew at work than there had been. It was the same for the next three days. Jerry joined him on the work details, saying it kept his mind off of his wife.

Joshua looked up from the deck as he was running the next day and saw a roughness to the horizon in front of the ship. They were approaching land.

After breakfast the public address system chimed and the Captain began speaking. "Ladies and Gentlemen, I am pleased to announce that we will be making landfall in the morning at Savanna, Georgia. We have had contact with amateur radio operators that say, though the city was hit with a nuclear missile, it missed the port. The radioactivity is down enough to allow a small volunteer crew to go in and look for fuel and food. We will not be able to remain. Everyone will be transferred to the life boats, which will remain offshore to avoid the radiation until the ship can refuel and restock if fuel and provisions are available."

There were loud protests all around Joshua. Seems most of the people wanted to go to shore as soon as possible. Jerry looked over at Joshua. "What do you think? You going to try to get to shore?"

"Are you nuts? Right into a radiation zone? No way."

Someone behind them had heard Joshua's comment. "You don't know what you're talking about, fellow. He said the radiation was low enough to go in. He wouldn't be doing that if there was any real risk. He just wants to get us off the ship so they can get the food and fuel and for themselves so they can go back to England.”

“If there is no risk, why don’t you ask to go in with the ship and disembark? Head out on your own.”

“I think I’ll do just that, smart guy!” The man stomped off, looking for a ship’s officer.

“You sure, Josh?” Jerry asked.

“Sure as I can be. I think the Captain and most of the crew has done everything they could to keep us safe. I’m not going to start questioning them now.”

“Okay. I’m with you, then.”

Apparently quite a few of the passengers and crew had the same idea as the angry man, for the Captain was on the public address system only a few minutes later with another announcement. You could hear the anger in his voice. “Ladies and Gentlemen. This is not a game. Several of us, all volunteers, will be risking our future health in trying to re-supply the Elite in order to get to a place that is safe enough for us all. No one will be allowed to disembark from the ship at the port. That is all.”

There were more outcries. Joshua and Jerry got out of the crowd, suddenly fearing that violence might break out. They found a corner out of the way and watched the crowd warily. The ship began to slow and the report-to-lifeboats alarm sounded. Joshua and Jerry headed to their respective staterooms to get their life jackets and report to their lifeboat stations.

Joshua was amazed at how few people were coming out to the lifeboats. More people began to show up, but not nearly as quickly as they had at the lifeboat drill just a few days ago. It was almost twenty minutes before they began boarding the lifeboats. Joshua was sure not everyone had shown up by then. But his boat was full and being lowered to the water below and he lost sight of the activity on board the Elite.

As each lifeboat was filled to capacity, it was lowered, and motored out a little ways from the ship. They gathered together, keeping enough distance to avoid bumping into each other from the gentle wave action. The Elite began to move toward the opening to the harbor.

Suddenly a fight broke out in Joshua's lifeboat. Two men were trying to drag the helmsman down from his perch. One of them was another crewmember. Others were fighting to keep them from doing so. But more people joined those trying to take over the lifeboat. Joshua was sitting well away from the helm and was unable to influence the fight.

The helmsman was dragged down and passed hand over hand and thrown out the door of the lifeboat. The other crewman climbed onto the raised helmsman's perch. "We're going in," said the man that had helped drag the original helmsman down. "Anyone don't want to go can just get out now."

There were loud protests. Joshua was one of the first to head for the door of the lifeboat. He had to climb over several people to get there, but he did, and dived out into the water. He was followed by several more, but the rest that had protested fell silent. They weren't going into the water.

The new helmsman set off toward the shoreline. Everyone in the water began swimming toward another lifeboat. It started happening all over the small fleet of lifeboats when people saw the other one leaving the group. A couple more lifeboats broke away. There were people leaving other boats, swimming toward those departing. All but the first lifeboat stopped to pick up those that wanted to go to shore.

When it was obvious what was going on, people began to shift from lifeboat to lifeboat when one indicated the majority wanted to stay and another wanted to go. Joshua was amazed that a full three-quarters of the lifeboats headed for shore.

The lifeboats staying behind regrouped and redistributed people to ease overcrowding. It was getting dark when the Elite returned to the group of lifeboats. The crew aboard the ship reconnected the lift cables and pulled the lifeboats up to unload.

Joshua saw the Captain talking to one of the officers that had been with the lifeboats. Joshua could tell that he was both angry and disappointed. Many of those that had deserted had been crew. Joshua found out a little later from a talkative crewmember that several passengers had indeed stayed aboard in hiding and exited the ship when it docked and the gangway was lowered. As with the lifeboats, some crew left the Elite, too.

He found out why they hadn't moved after everyone was aboard. The Captain sent a select team to shore in one of the lifeboats to recover the others. Joshua went up on deck to watch. He saw the string of lifeboats coming back near midnight. The group had recovered all but three of the lifeboats.

When they were hoisted up and locked in their brackets the Elite got underway again. It wasn't long before the Captain was on the public address system. "Ladies and Gentlemen. I am pleased to announce that we are now fully fueled and have added significantly to our food stores. As you are all aware, I have lost many of my crew to desertion. Any passenger willing to help in the operation of this ship will be greatly appreciated.

"I am also pleased to announce that we located records at the harbor that a regular supply tanker load of diesel was inbound to the harbor from Houston, Texas. I plan to find that ship. That is all."

Joshua found many of the crew that had gone into Savanna Harbor, including a few of the officers, were more talkative than in the past. He got most of the story of what had gone on in the harbor and in the recovery of the lifeboats.

There was a great deal of damage in the harbor from the blast and ground waves of the device that hit on the western edge of Savanna. Those on the bridge of the ship could see the devastation extending to the limit of their line of sight. The tanks in the tank farm for the harbor all seemed to be standing. There were several empty berths available and the crew docked the ship and then went ashore to see if they could get the fueling system going so they could re-fuel the Elite.

It took most of the day for the work crew assigned to the fuel to find a generator and hook it up to the pump feeding the fuel line to their berth. Though the tanks had appeared undamaged from a distance, when the crew got there they discovered quite a bit of damage. But there was some diesel fuel suitable for the engine in the Elite available in one tank. They transferred all they could get out of the tank to the ship.

While the one team was working on the fuel, two more were sent in search of useable food, with the caution not to venture too far from the harbor. They were able to get a couple of forklifts running, as well as one semi-truck.

They scoured the harbor area for delivery trucks. Much of the food they found had been fresh and was now a rotting mess. But there were canned, bottled and packaged foods, as well. They gathered up all they could find. Like the fuel, there was a limited amount. But it would feed the ship's complement for at least two weeks, they decided, if it was rationed carefully. And they still had a week's worth aboard. They loaded everything aboard, including the forklift that ran on diesel, after strengthening the boarding ramp to the cargo hold. Just in case it was needed in the future.

When it was discovered that three quarters of the passengers and half of the crew had deserted, and the Captain had decided not to try to force those that had left back aboard the ship, he received updated estimates on their situation. They had food for a month for those left aboard, and the fuel tanks were almost full. Since the ship was equipped with desalinators, they didn't have to worry about water, as long as they had fuel.

Joshua was watching through the windows on the lifeboat deck when those that were going after the other lifeboats disembarked. He noticed that two of the men carried shotguns. They were the ones used for shooting trap off the aft deck. The Captain was not playing games with the deserters. They could leave, but they weren't taking any more of the ship's property than he could help.

It didn't take long to find the lifeboats, bright orange that they were, clustered together near the south shore of the harbor. Apparently those in three of the lifeboats had decided on another location. The recovery crew was able to transfer helmsmen to the other craft and left, without ever seeing anyone ashore, not even a campfire. No one was even standing a watch on the lifeboats. A couple of them weren't even tied up to the shore, but were drifting free, a quarter of a mile away.

CHAPTER THREE

The Captain headed the Elite south, keeping the ship just within visual range of the coast. A constant radar watch was kept to try and locate the wayward tanker if it was still at sea. Every time they saw signs of life ashore they halted and checked it out. Carefully. Twice the launch was fired upon before it got close to shore. The other times it was small bands of people eager to get aboard the ship.

Joshua was curious why the Captain wouldn't let anyone else aboard. He overheard two of the officers discussing it. It was because of the reports they were getting of the levels of fallout along most areas of the coast. Most of those people that weren't staying in shelters were going to die, most sooner, some later.

They tried stopping at a couple of the small towns and cities, to try to find additional food, but were rebuffed each time by the residents. Armed residents. Seemed that if the place was habitable, then the residents didn't want any more drain on their resources and if it was abandoned it was still too hot to enter. As it was, those that had gone into Savanna Harbor suffered mild symptoms of radiation poisoning.

There were cruising slowly, just passing Hobe Sound when the sentry on binocular duty called into the bridge. "I see something. It's definitely a tanker."

The Elite made a sweeping turn and headed for the sound. The ship lay at anchor some distance from shore. The ship's launch was grounded nearby on shore. There were no signs of life on shore or aboard the Giuseppe when

Elite crew checked each one out. There were signs of heavy fallout, though rains after the fall had washed most of it off the decks of the ship.

Captain Bainseborough-Smith sent a team from the engineering section to see if they could get the ship in operating condition. It didn't take long. Essentially it had been parked and the key turned off. Everything fired right up. With a couple of engineering crew aboard the Captain brought the others back and transferred enough operations crew to handle the ship.

Fearful of the radiation, the Captain took both ships back out to sea. While it wasn't a super tanker by any means, the Giuseppe's cargo tanks could keep both ships sailing the area for several years.

It was obvious, from both direct observation and reports from amateur radio operators that had survived, that the peninsula of Florida was a washout as far as replenishing the ships food stocks. With fuel not a problem, the Captain set the ships' course south to the Caribbean.

They were able to replenish food supplies about as quickly as they consumed them. Those that had stayed aboard were committed to staying aboard. Those that had it contributed money and belongings to the Elite's bank to purchase what wasn't just lying around as they visited island after island. It was usually from small farmers away from the regular port cities.

They were not welcome in many places, especially those that already had a cruise ship or two at berth. The Giuseppe was always left out of sight of land with guards on board armed with shotguns when the Elite went in to shore try to bargain for supplies. It seemed many of the cruise ships were doing the same thing. Pickings were slim. And the demand for the Giuseppe fuel was high when it was discovered to be traveling with the Elite. The Captain headed them toward South America to stay out of harm's way.

Stops were made every few days all along the Central American east coast. Additional food stocks were purchased from the locals, using anything and everything not tied down to the ship, including the clothing and possessions the deserters had left behind. When they reached Brazilian national waters they had more success, stocking up heavily on fresh food, including a great deal of meat that went into the ship's freezers. People quit asking what they were having for the next meal, when they got the answers to the questions the first time.

It went well until the Brazilian authorities found out about the Giuseppe. It was ordered into shore. The Brazilians sent a patrol boat out for it, but Captain Bainseborough-Smith ordered it to head due east as fast as it could go. He turned the Elite to follow.

Though the patrol boat caught up with the tanker it only circled it a few times and left. The only thing Joshua could think of was that the Brazilian's still had some infrastructure up and wasn't willing to spill blood over the tanker. But the Elite and Giuseppe were no longer welcome.

It was winter in the Southern Hemisphere. The Captain turned them back north. They were able to pick up food again along the northern shores of South America and the eastern shores of Central America. When they got to Mexico it was a near repeat of Brazil. They were ordered in, but when they didn't go, they were left alone.

They had accumulated three months' worth of food. They headed for Texas. They found a good source of beef in one of the little Texas towns near the shore. This time the Captain had to trade diesel for it, but they got more than a year's worth of beef and pork.

They'd taken on live chickens and goats when in South America, along with a great deal of feed, so had ongoing sources of chicken, eggs, and milk, to go along with the beef and pork that was butchered and frozen.

With those stocks of food, and the fish they were catching with tackle they'd traded for, they were good for well over a year. Now they needed a home base.

They found it in Louisiana near the Texas border. Houston and Galveston had been hammered with nuclear weapons, and with the other targets hit in Texas, the area received a great deal of fallout. But that was fading. There were very few residents left in the area. With the Captain's permission, most of the passengers and crew opted to stay aboard the Elite. It had everything they needed, except for an actual source for food.

With the two ships in a small, safe harbor, The Elite survivors set up a presence on shore. It took days of exploration on foot to locate a working vehicle. When they found one it allowed them to scavenge in the surrounding area. They found what they needed to prepare gardens, including seeds. The Captain took the ship back to Texas and got more beef. On the hoof this time, to start their own herd.

Joshua fretted, wanting to go look for Precious, but not willing to leave immediately. He felt a responsibility to help get a permanent presence set up on land. With the fuel they had they could live aboard ship as long as they had food. Joshua did what he could for the rest of that year and the next. During that time he bought a whole head of beef with his Rolex watch, and made arrangements with one of the chefs to cut it up for him using the ship's equipment, for the last of his cash.

He turned nearly an equal amount of the weight of the steer into beef jerky, trading other people specific cuts for more suitable cuts of meat to make into the jerky.

There were boats all along the coast for the taking.

Joshua couldn't believe his luck when he ran across a sunken MacGregor 26 power sailor on one of his first exploration journeys. Every once in a while, in his past life, he went through a phase of wanting a boat suitable for the Missouri lakes. He'd been impressed with the MacGregor. It was a decent sailor and very good under power. Though it was down to the gunnels in the water, the boat was unsinkable.

He checked under the water for damage and found none. He salvaged a small gasoline powered pump and pumped the boat out, and began refurbishing it in his spare time between his work assignments for the community.

The outboard motor that had been on the boat was ruined, but he found a brand new Mercury four stroke 15 hp outboard. It would do until he could get the boat to a good marina and find a 50 hp to up engine the boat. It would be awkward, but Joshua intended to keep the 15 hp on board for emergency use.

Joshua was able to find dozens of the standard 6-gallon and 12-gallon marine fuel tanks on other boats, but gasoline was scarce. He made sure there were a couple of siphons on board the boat.

With the boat and jerky ready the spring of the third year after the war, Joshua was ready to start his journey to find his daughter, Precious. Having said his good-bye's Joshua set sail eastward, headed for the mouth of the Mississippi.

He steered clear of any place that looked inhabited, but checked every place along the shore that looked abandoned. He was looking for gasoline, guns and ammunition, and a water purifier. He had water for a week or more on board, but he wanted a way to treat more.

It took a great deal of time, but Joshua's searches along the Louisiana sea coast, and then the Mississippi River banks finally paid off. He found gasoline here and there, and at one river marina, found an almost full case of 16-ounce bottles of PRI-G.

When he first saw the product he didn't know what it was, but when he checked the marina's fuel tanks there was a sign that suggested the PRI-G or PRI-D be used with all the marina's fuel. He went back into the marina store, got the one bottle they had on display and searched the back room until he found the rest of the case. He grabbed a couple of first-aid kits on display. He didn't have one.

Though he didn't need it for the MacGregor, Joshua intended to be traveling by land vehicle at some point and took all the PRI-D he could find, too. There was no telling what he might find that would run.

That marina was a treasure trove in other ways. He found a Mercury 50 hp outboard on one of the boats docked in the marina. It was a struggle, but he got it mounted on the MacGregor, with the 15 hp drained, cleaned, and stored on the foredeck. It would only be used if the 50 hp quit on him until he could find another.

The marina store also catered to campers and hikers in the area. They had a small selection of water purifiers. He took all they had, all the replacement filters he could find, and all the accessories. Also some camping equipment.

He began to find more gasoline along one stretch of the river. From what he could see, it had residual amounts of fallout. He saw nothing moving except for fish jumping in the river. With the small chance of someone being around, he searched a little more thoroughly for firearms when he came to nice looking properties facing the river.

Joshua found what he assumed was a World War II vet's house. It too, like the one marina, was a treasure trove. Joshua found the partially eaten human remains sitting in a chair in the living room of the house, an issue model Colt 1911 pistol in his hand. Propped nearby was an M1 Garand and a Winchester 97 12 gauge trench gun. Both the Garand and the shotgun had long bayonets attached.

The man had all the accoutrements.—cartridge box web belt and suspenders, with ammunition, holster and knife sheaths, a pair of canteens, and two double pouches for the 1911 magazines. There was also a butt pack, and a combat pack with entrenching tool and a machete strapped to it. The two packs were empty. A full dozen 80-round bandoleers with loaded ammunition in the Garand en-bloc clips where at hand. Joshua was doubtful that they were issue, but there were two fifty round leather bandoleers of 12 gauge 00 buck hanging on the top spindle of the chair.

Joshua searched the rest of the house. He found more ammunition for all three weapons stashed in a closet. There was also quite a bit of canned and packaged food. Joshua took it all. He made five trips from the house to the MacGregor, worried each step that he was staying in one place too long. But still he checked behind the house. Sure enough, there was a restored Willys Jeep. It had a D-handle shovel under one door opening and an axe under the other, and a spare tire and fuel can on the rear. Joshua took the tools and fuel can. It was full. He checked the shed. Six more cans of fuel.

He debated taking the jeep, but it was on the wrong side of the river, and he doubted he could make as good of time northward in the Jeep as he could the boat. Not to mention finding enough gasoline. He was in good shape now, with all his marine portable tanks full and the seven cans from the vet, a dangerous amount, in normal circumstances. He had fuel stashed all over the boat.

After he had loaded everything aboard, Joshua motored away at high speed. The place was giving him the willies.

Joshua was stopping in the heaviest cover he could along the banks for his night stops. He saw the occasional boat out, mostly rowboats, but none showed an inclination to contact him, other than a casual wave as he sailed past. He picked up sailing skills fairly rapidly, though he was far from being an expert.

He was motoring along a stretch of the river with many twists and turns when he met a big jon boat coming down stream under paddle power. The two men in the boat were as startled as Joshua. Joshua looked back. The jon boat was going around the bend. But then he heard the motor that was mounted on the boat fire up and the boat came rushing back around the bend, under full power.

The man in the front of the boat lifted a shotgun and began to fire at the MacGregor. Joshua slammed the throttle of the Mercury 50 hp and sped away. The jon boat, though up on plane, couldn't keep up with the MacGregor at full speed, as the jon boat's engine began to sputter and then died, leaving them languishing in the MacGregor's wake.

Joshua wiped the sweat off his brow and thought to check himself, the boat, and the engines for damage. From the looks of the pellet marks, the man had been using small shot. There were indentations on the motor housings and marks on the back of the boat. It was only when he turned back to face forward that he realized he taken a pellet in his left arm.

He waited until he found a place with a lot of overhanging vegetation, lowered the mast, and eased under it. Then he tended the wound. It wasn't bad, but Joshua didn't want it to fester. After sterilizing the blade of his pen knife, Joshua dug out the pellet. It hurt like the dickens, but Joshua managed to get the pellet out without screaming, but it was a near thing.

Wishing he had some alcohol, to wash out the wound as well as to use as a painkiller, he put a Band-Aid on the little hole and then extricated the MacGregor from the foliage and headed north again, at speed, until he decided he was far enough ahead of the jon boat that it wouldn't be able to catch him, even if they got their outboard going again.

Joshua kept his vigilance up as he traveled, keeping to the center of the river. There were places where people were on shore, and long stretches with no evidence of anyone. He had two more incidents of being shot at, but he was able to motor away with no damage.

He kept stopping at abandoned places along the river and continued to find small amounts of gasoline, and even some food to supplement his jerky. He used the sail whenever he could, to lessen fuel consumption, but he was fighting the downstream current all the time.

Joshua couldn't figure out the apparent huge amounts of fallout that seemed to cover the ground in many places after he passed the southern border of Arkansas. It just didn't look right to be radioactive fallout. Finally, somewhat against his better judgment, he pulled ashore at a place that was covered in the material. He picked up a handful. It wasn't radioactive fallout, it was volcanic ash. Their shipboard amateurs had mentioned that Yellowstone had blown, but he hadn't given it much credence at the time. He was a believer now.

Finally he got close to St. Louis. His initial plan had been to stop below St. Louis, a probable target in the war, find a useable vehicle and go over land the rest of the way. But the more he thought about it, going past St. Louis and taking the Missouri upstream seemed to be a better idea. The MacGregor was doing well. If he could get past St. Louis on the Mississippi, and then take the Missouri River, he could go all the way to Kansas City by water. Another potential nuclear target was Jefferson City, Missouri, the state capital. It was right on the Missouri River.

Joshua decided to at least try to get to the Missouri. He searched for more gas, and managed to fill his containers again, this time from abandoned cars on the highways adjacent to the river. His siphon hose worked like a charm. All he had to do was punch through the anti-siphon block in the filler necks of the newer cars, and siphon the fuel into cans.

He began to see an oily sheen on the surface of the river the closer he got to St. Louis. He began to see damage to the structures near the river. He brought the MacGregor to a halt, using the engine to just hold him in place against the current. It took a couple of minutes to make up his mind. Joshua switched to a full 12-gallon fuel tank and ran the throttle up to full speed. He stayed on the east side of the river, though well away from the shore.

He had to slow down to navigate across the fallen river bridges. Everyone in the St. Louis area was down. Joshua saw no one as he motored past the destroyed city.

He saw the tanks right on the bank that were leaking diesel into the river. There was probably plenty of gas in one of those tank farms, but he was afraid the radiation levels would be too high for safety.

Joshua had a tense moment when he came to the Alton, Illinois Dam and locks. If they were closed, he didn't know if he would be able to get past them. But his worries faded when he saw clear passage. He motored through and past, and then into the mouth of the Missouri. He felt ill after traveling two days up the Missouri and laid low for a couple. He couldn't keep anything on his stomach for the entire two days. Most of his nausea resulted in dry heaves after that.

But he felt better after another day, though rather weak. Joshua admitted to himself that he'd received a pretty good radiation dose passing St. Louis. A week later he began losing some of his thick shock of hair, but it didn't last long. He was seeing more people now, despite the evidence of the heavy ash fall.

He began to approach people, his acquired weapons at hand. He was able to trade for some fresh food at one place, for some of his jerky, and another place some gasoline for jerky. He sheared away quickly from anyone that showed any signs of aggression. He was a tempting target and knew it. Most of the other boats he was seeing on the river were much smaller.

If Jefferson City had been a target, it had been missed. He sailed past without a problem. He was on the last leg of the journey. Joshua was dismayed when he reached the northeast corner of the city. It was as close to the city as he could get on the boat. It wasn't looking good and he began to worry about radiation.

He found a good spot and unloaded the boat onto shore. He buried the fuel and most of the food in several caches, including one that contained the Winchester 97. Then he hooked up the pump he'd used to raise the MacGregor and used it to sink her again.

He buried the pump, using a piece of tarp he'd scavenged one day, with no particular use in mind. It just seemed a boat needed tarps. With the camping equipment in and on the combat pack and butt pack, and food and water inside, Joshua holstered the Colt and picked up the Garand. He didn't get very far. From the looks of the destruction, one of the detonations had not been very far away. And in that direction were the remains of his home. It might even be at ground zero.

There was nothing there for him. He turned back, tears in his eyes. If Precious was alive, there were no clues on how to find her. In the four days he'd been on foot, nothing had changed where he'd stashed the MacGregor. He raised the boat, dug up his gear and loaded it back aboard, and then set sail.

Several times Joshua thought about stopping and trying to make a life for himself in one of the communities he was passing for the second time. But the weather was extremely cool for the time of the year and Joshua knew the cruise ship encampment on the gulf was going to be the best chance he had of long term survival.

He wasted no time going back. The current was with him all the way He picked up a bullet in the shoulder from the Louisiana side of the Mississippi when he was about halfway down the state. Joshua was in bad shape when he grounded the MacGregor at the cruise ship encampment and waded ashore three days later.

The next thing he remembered was waking up in the ship's infirmary, with Patricia holding his hand. He became an expert fisherman, with the MacGregor his fishing vessel. It looked a bit puny next to some of the other, diesel powered boats that had been salvaged. But they were on rationed amounts of diesel from the tanker. Joshua could go out anytime he wanted, under sail, which was often.

He was able to keep his fuel tanks full, trading fish. Someone somewhere close was rumored to have found a gasoline tanker and pup. Joshua didn't care where the gasoline came from. He filled every container he could find, treating the fuel with PRI-G, to have the fuel for a rainy day. Despite the warnings from those that knew about the amount of gasoline he had onboard the MacGregor, he continued to store it on the boat.

Another thing that Joshua did was get married to Patricia. The Captain performed the ceremony, for them and three other couples that had formed. Two of the other brides, and one of the grooms were locals.

Joshua settled in with Patricia in the same stateroom he'd had on the ship, and while she tended garden and helped in the kitchen and with the children, Joshua fished. He lost track of time, except for what season it was. And wondered about his Precious. He just knew she was alive somewhere.

But the tranquility came to an end one afternoon. Joshua was well out into the gulf. Patricia had come along for the ride that day, with the garden in good shape. But the fish weren't biting, no matter what bait or lure Joshua used. Even the mascot porpoise that often traveled with the boat for the occasional piece of fish that Joshua would toss to it was nowhere to be found.

"I think we might as well go in," Joshua said, reeling in first one line and then the other three. Patricia got behind the wheel and Joshua began raising the sail.

Suddenly Joshua felt a sinking sensation in his stomach. Apparently Patricia had the same feeling. "Did you feel that, Josh?"

"Yeah. But what was it?" Joshua had the sail up and they began to head for the distant shore. They hadn't gone very far when their radio came alive. "Tsunami! Tsunami! Can you hear me, Joshua? Tsunami!" It was Tom Jones, one of the radio operators on the Elite. A communications watch was always kept when anyone was away from the group.

Joshua keyed the mike of the radio when he got to it. "This is Joshua. I hear you man! Are you sure?"

"Oh, yeah! The sea just started flowing away. We're trying to get the ships to deep water. Let us know if you experience a surge. How far out are you?"

"Twenty miles," Joshua replied. "We felt something, but it wasn't like a surge. More like a drop."

"Holy cow!" exclaimed Tom. "If you're getting it out there already it must be huge!" There was silence for a moment. "But that doesn't seem reasonable, if it doing it there and here at the same time. But never mind. Just keep an eye out."

It was generations before scientists pieced together what had happened that day and several subsequent days. A tectonic movement of epic proportions had snapped the North American Tectonic Plate in two from deep in the Gulf of Mexico up the Mississippi River Valley and over to the Great Lakes and the St. Lawrence Seaway.

For eons the bedrock deep under the center of the United States had been stretched thinner and thinner, resulting in the Reelfoot Rift. The surface would have sunk with the bedrock, except billions of tons of eroded rock coming from the Rockies and the Appalachians, and even the Ozarks, had filled the sunken land in, just slightly slower than the ground was sinking.

When the plate separated magma began to stream upward in hundreds of places. But it was still deep in the earth and much of it cooled and hardened quickly, sealing the crack except for here and there. A new line of volcanoes arose along the length of the split.

The waters of the Gulf of Mexico flowed northward over the sunken ground, stopping only when it reached Cape Girardeau, Missouri in the north, the Ozarks in the west, and the foothills of the Appalachians to the east. The Gulf of Mexico was now the American Sea.

Water flowed from the Atlantic into the new sea, and the Pacific flowed into the Atlantic. It took years for the oceans to equalize. In that time old currents disappeared and new ones were created.

CHAPTER FOUR

Joshua brought the sails down and secured them and then got behind the wheel after Patricia moved. She went down into the cabin and brought out life preservers for both of them. Joshua put his on and then started the Mercury. He put it in gear, but just let the engine idle. He wanted to be able to head into the swell, no matter from which direction it came. But they never felt a swell.

The crews of both the Elite and the Giuseppe weren't sure they would get the ships under power and moving before they touched bottom. But the Gulf quit withdrawing and began to edge back, but not with a swell they were expecting.

Not one to take a chance, Captain Bainseborough-Smith ordered both ships out to sea at full speed as soon as they had way. People on shore ran for the gangplank of the Elite when the public address system was activated and warnings rang out. If it was a tsunami they had no high ground to run up on this stretch of coast.

When the crew saw the last person close aboard the ship they pulled up the gangway. Other people began to show up, but the Captain ordered the gangway kept up. Those still coming from the gardens headed for the small fleet of boats tied up to the shore.

Several noticed the water was slowly rising up the shore, but there didn't seem to be anything but normal wave action. It was just that every wave went a little further up the beach. The small boats all began pulling away from the shore, the last one waiting for the last person to get to it.

Both ships and all the boats were well clear of the little harbor when everyone felt a strange sensation. It was like they were going backwards, with the ship tilted slightly. But they weren't getting any closer to the shoreline. In fact, the shore was receding from them rapidly. It was only when people saw that the water had crossed the nearest small rise and the ground kept going underwater that they realized that the water wasn't just moving on to the land. The land itself seemed to be sinking.

A bridge crewman looked at the radar display and let out a yelp. The coastline was disappearing at a rapid pace. Very soon they wouldn't be able to see it and the ships were not moving that fast yet for the shore to be disappearing. The boats were well out ahead of them, being able to accelerate much faster than the ships.

The ships had a radar bearing on Joshua's boat and both ships and the boats headed in that direction. They rendezvoused with him and then stopped dead in the water to wait out whatever was happening. Though, like Joshua, everyone kept engines at idle, ready to engage and meet the tsunami wave if it ever developed. It didn't all that day or the next one.

The Captain kept everyone apprised of the radar reports. When the land fell off the display, the ships and boats began to head back north. Cautiously. Keeping just within radar range of the land for a little while. Then they couldn't keep up with the submersion. There was some fear that they would run aground, but they kept going, the small boats in advance, watching the depth of the water with their depth sounders.

They began to see all sorts of items in the water as they continued following the receding shoreline. That included bodies. Dozens at a time, at times. Others singularly. Always bodies, never survivors. They steered wide around two new volcanoes that were building in their path. It took several days to reach the new shoreline.

There were people at the shore when the cruise ship approached. When asked where they were, those on shore told the ship's residents that the nearest city was Cape Girardeau, Missouri. Just to their east.

After the shock wore off, the locals objected to having 500 plus additional residents. The Captain decided to go west, on a whim. It was a good decision. They traveled until they found another, very new, safe harbor, at the edge of the Missouri Ozarks, near the submerged city of Doniphan. They put down new roots, figuratively and literally. New late season gardens were planted, and the surrounding forested hills were explored and the bounty that was available utilized. They began to make contact with the locals.

The Elite survivors settled in for the long haul. Again.

CHAPTER FIVE

Brady Collingsworth, with his wife and son, were leading the small convoy in their highly modified Suburban. Brady's and Star's adopted daughter had stayed behind to keep their garden going. Behind them were two heavily laden U500 Unimog trucks. Next in line was a ten-wheel tanker truck with diesel and gasoline. Behind the tanker came an assortment of old and even older pickup trucks. Every vehicle was pulling a trailer of some kind, just as heavily loaded as the tow vehicles.

If looking close, one would see that every person was heavily armed, with the exception of little Joshua Brady Collingsworth. There had not been any major problems with bandits in and around Branson for over a year, but Brady was not one to take chances. They were going into new territory, for them.

They had started from their retreat compound northwest of Branson, Missouri, picked up US 65 going north and cut across on highway F to Walnut Shade, where they picked up US 160 going east. That was the limit they'd gone in their earlier explorations. From Walnut Shade east was new territory for them, post war.

The roads were rough in places, not having had much, if any maintenance since the War. The convoy traveled slowly for that reason, as well as security concerns. So far, thankfully, no major bridges had been out. They stopped early each evening to make camp. Two or three people would hunt in the surrounding forest, to add to the stock of food they brought with them. Most stops the hunters would come back with two or three squirrels or rabbits, or both. Occasionally there were a few ducks or pigeons. On the third day Brady got a deer.

Brady had the most luck bringing in game. When hunting he carried a Heym Model 37V vierling. A double barrel twenty-gauge with .308 and .22 Hornet rifle barrels under the shotgun barrels. It had been his wife's fathers. He could take anything with it efficiently that he ran across.

They didn't worry about game laws any more, just conservation. There had been a time, right after the war and the ash fall from Yellowstone that game had been nearly non-existent. But the game from other areas began to migrate to the area after a couple of years had passed. They had been careful not to over hunt their local area, to allow the game to become well established.

It took them almost a month of slow traveling on US 160 to reach their destination. As has been said about many roads, US 160 was long and winding.

The destination was the new coastline they'd heard about through the amateur radio operator network that had developed after the war for the survivors of the war to maintain communications. A much smaller network now, after the Yellowstone eruption and then the Great New Madrid Subsidence that had turned the Gulf of Mexico into the American Sea, the network had reported that the eastern edge of the Ozarks was now the northwest coast of the inverted-V shaped new sea.

Brady and the members of his convoy could attest that it was a fact. If they hadn't stopped short, they would have run right into it, since US 160 dipped into the water and disappeared. They were just west of where Doniphan, Missouri used to be. What was left of Doniphan was now underneath fifty feet of water.

When Brady cleared the last ridge before the sea he stopped in awe. Some of it was the sea itself. The rest of it was the fact that a small flotilla of ships and boats were moored and anchored in a small harbor that now existed where US 160 ended.

"I can't believe it," Brady said. "A cruise ship and tanker. It has to be some that were in the Gulf or the Caribbean when the balloon went up."

"It sure makes me feel better about Daddy," Star said, holding up Joshua to see the sea. "If one cruise ship survived, maybe Daddy's did too."

Joshua waved his arms and gurgled. He'd seen enough of the sea. It was time to be fed. Star took care of that as Brady led the convoy down the incline. He saw a suitable spot and had the vehicles pull up behind him and park, just off the road in an open area.

People were running from the ship and the surrounding forest to meet them. Several of Brady's group began to lift weapons, but Brady waved for them to put them down. The only sign of a weapon was the over-and-under shotgun a man near the edge of the forest held.

"Who are you and where'd you come from?" asked the first person to reach Brady, who was standing by the front corner of the Suburban.

"I could ask the same thing," Brady said, as his hand was shaken violently by the first man. Others gathered around.

"Perhaps we should take the visitors to visit the Captain," said another man. He exuded authority. The rest of the group opened up a lane toward the boats on the shore. "He can hear the story and then give an announcement."

"I'm Brady Collingsworth," Brady said, taking the man's hand with it was offered.

"I'm Lieutenant Robertson, of the Cruise Ship Elite. I'll take you to see the Captain."

"Is there a place we can set up camp?"

"Sure," Lieutenant Robertson said. He waved a hand toward the tree line. "Anywhere over there."

Brady turned back to his group, now gathered about the vehicles. "Hang loose and set up the camp," he told them. "I'm going to meet with this group's leader." He stuck his head in the open window of the Suburban. "You coming?" he asked Star.

"No. Still feeding the baby. Get the story and then tell me. And look out at that blue trimmed boat coming in. Daddy wanted one like that at one time."

"Thought about him a lot, lately, haven't you?"

"Yeah. I miss him. I hope he is okay."

"If he is as resourceful as you, I'm sure he's okay. I'll be back in a little while." Brady turned and went with the Lieutenant.

When he returned a shy hour later, the camp was all set up. The group was well practiced, from the weeks of travel. "It's incredible," Brady told the assembled group." He told the story, much the way that the Captain was telling people aboard the ship about Brady's group.

By the time Brady had finished the telling, people were streaming off the ship to meet Brady's group and get some of the story first hand. Brady's group felt the same way. Introductions began as the basic story was embellished with personal accounts by those in both groups.

"I want you to meet the Captain," Brady told Star, after going over to the Suburban. "He's a remarkable fellow. He's been keeping this bunch going and prospering since the war." They were walking toward the ship and Star's attention was drawn to the blue trimmed MacGregor 26 as the man and woman aboard finally disembarked. There was something about the man that looked familiar.

"I'm sorry. What did you say? I was distracted," Star said, turning back to Brady.

"I was saying, the Captain has been keeping this bunch going and prospering since the war."

"I heard that part," Star said, with a smile for her husband.

"Oh. Yeah. They were just starting out on a world cruise from New York when…"

Brady saw Star go pale. "New York? It can't be!" She whirled around to look at the man and woman walking up to them. Quickly she handed little Joshua to Brady and began running toward the man and woman approaching. "Daddy! Daddy! Is that you?"

"Precious?" Joshua asked softly. Then he was running toward Star. "It is you!"

Brady walked over, dumb founded, as several other people gathered around to see what the shouting was about.

Star was in Joshua's arms, laughing and crying at the same time as he swung her around and around. "I knew it!" Joshua said. "I was sure you were alive. I've been so worried about you."

"And I you. Put me down. I want to introduce you to someone." Star took little Joshua from Brady and handed him to her father. "This is Joshua Brady Collingsworth, your grandson."

"Grandson? You're married?" Joshua stared at the baby.

"Well, no ceremony, but in our eye's and our group's eyes, we are," Star said. "This is Brady. My husband."

Joshua cradled little Joshua in his left arm and shook Brady's hand. "It looks like you are taking good care of my Precious. Thank you."

"She doesn't take much caring for. She's been a big part of our group's success. And we call her Star."

"Star?" Joshua asked, looking over at his daughter.

Star blushed. "Long story. It doesn't matter. You can still call me Precious."

"I guess I should introduce you to Patricia," Joshua said, noticing Star's eyes flicking toward the woman standing just to the side and behind him.

"This is Patricia. She's my wife. The Captain married us."

"What happened to Sue?" Star asked.

A grim look crossed Joshua's face. "Another long story. We didn't last long together after the war started. She got off with a bunch of the others at Savanna."

"Savanna is on the hot list," Brady said.

"I know. We're part of an amateur radio network. They're keeping track of things."

"We're in it, too," Brady said.

"Small world," Joshua commented.

Brady looked at Star and then Joshua. "I hope to tell ya'." He laughed. "Oh, yes. I have something you might want back." With Star and Patricia talking, Brady took Joshua over to the Suburban and brought out the vierling case.

"My Vierling! You saved it."

"Yes. Star brought it along. I've been using it hunting. Great gun. I'm sure you'll want it back."

Joshua began to shake his head. "No. No, I'm a fisherman. You keep it and use it. And then pass it down to your son. Something like that should be a family heirloom." He looked down. Little Joshua had fallen asleep.

"Why… Why thank you, Joshua. I will do as you suggest. Thank you."

EPILOGUE

It didn't take long for Brady's group, with the cruise ship residents' help, to erect the two steel Quonset style buildings they dismantled in Branson and brought with them.

Brady and the Captain talked again. It wasn't difficult to hammer out a mutual aid agreement. Brady's group and the other retreat groups in the MAG would trade fresh produce and meat to supplement the ship's gardens. They would also arm several of the residents, just in case more trouble developed, and as an aid to hunting. One of the first animals to make a comeback had been feral hogs and razorbacks. The shotguns the ship had weren't doing that well on them.

The residents of the ship agreed that they would provide frozen seafood to the MAGs if a semi with a reefer trailer could be found. Brady told the Captain that it wouldn't be a problem. Brady had already found three. Two were being used for refrigerated storage at the retreat. The other would be used for the round trips carrying food between the areas. If they could find a fourth, they would just swap filled trailers each trip. They would split the fuel usage.

As the weeks passed, and then months, the populations of the ship and the various Ozark retreats merged and inter-married. Life would go on.

The End

THANK YOU FOR READING "OZARK RETREAT"

By

Jerry D. Young

LIKE THIS BOOK?

See more great books at www.creativetexts.com

"SIMPLER TIMES"
"BUGGING HOME"
"THE SLOW ROAD"
"LOW PROFILE"
"RUDY'S PREPAREDNESS SHOP"
"CME: CORONAL MASS EJECTION"
"HOME SWEET BUNKER"
"THE HERMIT"

& MANY MORE GREAT
POST-APOCALYPTIC FICTION
& OTHER TITLES

THANK YOU!